"Does that mean you'll take the job?"

"I'd love it," said Prue honestly, "but...well, I don't have that much experience of babies. Wouldn't you rather have someone more qualified?" She grimaced, thinking of the catalog of mistakes she'd made since she'd been at Cowen Creek, let alone the rest of her life. "Someone more efficient?"

"I'd rather have someone like you," Nat said. "You're a nice girl," he added gruffly. "You love the Outback and you want to come back. Those are all good reasons as far as I'm concerned. And then, you need to go to London just when I do...."

"You could almost say that we're meant for each other!" Prue finished for him cheerfully. "I mean...jobwise," she added uncomfortably.

Nat flashed her an enigmatic look. "What else?" he said in a dry voice.

Strong and silent...
Powerful and passionate...
Tough and tender...

Who can resist the rugged loners of the Outback?
As tough and untamed as the land they rule,
they burn as hot as the Australian sun once they
meet the woman they've been waiting for!

Look out for more AUSTRALIANS
throughout 2002 in Harlequin Romance®!

Coming in July:
Strategy for Marriage (#3707)
by bestselling Australian author of more than 80 novels,
Margaret Way

If you'd like to find out more about Jessica Hart,
you can visit her Web site www.jessicahart.co.uk

Men who turn your whole world upside down!

INHERITED: TWINS!

Jessica Hart

TORONTO • NEW YORK • LONDON
AMSTERDAM • PARIS • SYDNEY • HAMBURG
STOCKHOLM • ATHENS • TOKYO • MILAN • MADRID
PRAGUE • WARSAW • BUDAPEST • AUCKLAND

ISBN 0-373-03701-5

INHERITED: TWINS!

First North American Publication 2002.

CHAPTER ONE

PRUE was slumped miserably over the steering wheel when the sound of an approaching vehicle made her jerk upright. At last! Scrambling out of the car, she saw a utility truck bowling along the track towards her, a cloud of red dust billowing behind it.

Too tired to realise that the car was effectively blocking the track on its own, she began to wave her arms frantically and even though she knew that no one in the outback would drive past a vehicle in trouble, she felt weak with relief as the ute slowed and stopped at last a few feet in front of her.

The driver wound down his window and leant out. 'You look like you could use some help,' he said in a laconic voice.

He had a quiet, pleasant face that was vaguely familiar. Prue groped desperately for his name. Nat... Nat *something* was the best she could do. He was one of the Grangers' neighbours, if you could really call anyone who lived seventy miles away a neighbour.

'Hello,' she greeted him, wincing inwardly at how clipped and English she sounded compared to his slow Australian drawl. Taking her sunglasses off, she bent down to look at him through the window, and Nat found himself looking back into a pair of silvery-grey eyes that bore distinct traces of tears on the long, sooty lashes.

'I can't tell you how glad I am to see you!' she said. 'I was beginning to wonder if I'd be here all night!'

Nat switched off the engine and got out of the ute. He

was a rangy man in his thirties, with the spare, self-contained look that Prue had grown used to seeing in the outback.

'It's Prue, isn't it?' he said, settling his hat on his head.

Prue looked at him in surprise. 'That's right.'

'I'm Nat Masterman.'

Masterman, that was it! 'Oh, I know,' she said hastily. 'I remember you coming to Cowen Creek. I was just surprised that you recognised me. Not many people notice a cook.'

Nat was puzzled himself to have remembered her so clearly. She was slight with a cloud of brown hair and a face that was piquant rather than pretty. He hadn't noticed that much about her on the few occasions he had seen her, only her eyes, which were an unusual silver colour, and the way she had lit up whenever Ross Granger smiled at her.

'That depends on how good the cook is,' he said tactfully. 'You made the best apple pie I've ever had.'

'Really?' Prue smiled at him gratefully. It was nice to think that she was good at something. 'Thank you!'

Yes, he had noticed her smile, too, Nat remembered. He adjusted the brim of his hat. 'What's the trouble, Prue?' he asked.

Reminded of her situation, Prue's smile faded. 'I've run out of diesel,' she said glumly.

Nat's brow rose slightly. 'Are you sure?'

She nodded. 'The red warning light has been blinking at me for miles, but by the time I noticed it I'd gone too far to go back. I was hoping to get to the sealed road at least—' she went on, kicking one of the tyres in remembered frustration '—but the engine started to cough and splutter just up the track, and then it just died.'

She blew her fringe wearily off her face. 'I've been here over two hours.'

It felt more than twice as long.

Prue saw Nat glance at her curiously and was suddenly acutely aware of what a mess she must appear. There were plenty of ways to look good, but being stuck in a car in the middle of the outback for a couple of hours was certainly not one of them.

It might not have been so bad if there had been any shade where she could sit and wait, but out here on the salt pans she had had no choice but to stay in the car. The air-conditioning had died with the engine, and even with all the windows down the sun beating on the metal roof had soon turned the car into an oven. Now, her face was red and blotchy and her curls clung limp and sweaty to her scalp.

Rubbing a knuckle under her eyes to remove any tell-tale tear-stains and hastily replacing her sunglasses, Prue could only hope that she didn't look as if she had spent the last two hours snivelling pathetically, even if it *were* true.

Not that Nat Masterman seemed to care what she looked like. He was more concerned with the fuel situation. 'These things have got pretty big tanks,' he said, nodding his head at the car, a powerful four-wheel drive far bigger than anything Prue had ever driven at home. 'It must have been just about empty before you left Cowen Creek.'

'I know—and, yes, I know I should have checked it before I left,' said Prue, forestalling him as he opened his mouth. 'It was one of the first things the Grangers told me when I came to work out here.

'The thing is, I'd had a really busy morning,' she tried to explain her carelessness, 'and I suddenly realised that we were out of flour and sugar and a whole lot of other things I need to cook the meal tonight. I reckoned I had just enough time to get into town and back before I had to start cooking, so I just jumped in the car and set off. I was thinking about…other things…and, well, I just forgot,' she admitted.

And now here she was in another fine mess. Bitterly, Prue remembered the moment when the flashing red light had finally caught her eye, yanking her out of a wonderful daydream where Ross was marvelling at how they had ever managed at Cowen Creek without her.

He wouldn't be marvelling tonight when he found out that she had spent the afternoon stranded halfway to Mathison and that there would be no pudding. She had planned to make his favourite, too.

Prue was suddenly close to tears. 'I can't believe I could be so *stupid*!' she said fiercely, knowing that there was no one to blame but herself.

'Not so stupid that you left the car and tried to walk.'

Nat's voice was calm and insensibly comforting, and Prue looked at him gratefully. He might not be the type to make her go weak at the knees, like Ross, but he had always seemed like a nice man. Not that exciting, maybe, but quietly competent. If she had to be stranded in the middle of nowhere, she couldn't ask for anyone better to rescue her.

Not even Ross, she thought disloyally. Ross would know what to do, of course, but he wouldn't have been able to resist teasing her. Nat, she guessed, wouldn't tease, and he wouldn't rush to tell everyone how hopelessly unsuited she was to life in the outback either. He was the kind of man who only spoke when he had something important to say.

'I don't suppose you've got any spare diesel, have

you?' she asked him, hoping against hope that she would be able to avoid the ignominy of having to abandon the car altogether. If Nat had enough fuel to get her back to the homestead, she could make do for dinner and Ross might not ever have to know what had happened.

But Nat was already shaking his head. 'Sorry,' he said.

Prue tried, and failed, to swallow her disappointment. 'Oh, well.'

So much for Ross not finding out. She would have to go back and confess, that was all.

Squaring her shoulders, she flashed Nat a determinedly bright smile. 'Are you on your way to Cowen Creek?' she asked, even though she knew the question was unnecessary. Once on this track, there was nowhere else to go.

He nodded. 'I wanted to have a word with Bill Granger.'

'Would you give me a lift?'

'Sure,' Nat began, but something in her smile, something in the way she turned despondently back to the car to collect her things, made him pause. 'Unless you'd rather I took you into Mathison?' he heard himself offer.

Prue stopped with her hand on the car door. She looked at him with such amazement that Nat wondered if she had misunderstood what he had said. 'You could do your shopping while I get a can of fuel,' he explained. 'I'll bring you back here, and then you can drive yourself back to Cowen Creek.'

He made it sound perfectly simple, as if it was the most obvious thing in the world for him to go back on his tracks and drive an extra forty or so miles along hot, dusty roads for a girl he hardly knew.

'But...I thought you wanted to see Bill,' stammered Prue, unable to believe that the miracle she had spent the last two hours dreaming about would turn up in the shape of a lean, quiet grazier in a hat.

Nat shrugged. 'There's no hurry,' he said, incapable of explaining his impulsive offer to himself let alone to her.

No, there would never be a hurry as far as Nat Masterman was concerned, thought Prue enviously. He wouldn't know how to *begin* flapping or fussing or panicking. You could tell by the steadiness of his gaze, by the slowness of his voice, by the easy way he moved, that hurry was quite simply an alien concept for him.

'Even so, it would be taking you so far out of your way,' she said doubtfully.

'I don't mind,' he said. 'But if you'd rather I took you back to Cowen Creek—'

'No!' Prue interrupted him, determined not to let her opportunity go. 'I mean, if you're sure you don't mind, it would be *wonderful* if you could take me to Mathison!' she admitted, and her smile was so dazzling that Nat blinked and wondered how he could have thought that she wasn't particularly pretty.

He turned to open the door of the ute. 'Hop in, then,' he said in a dry voice.

Prue grabbed her hat and her shopping list from the car. She scrambled in beside him and collapsed back into the seat.

'You've saved my life!' she told him as he turned the ute with an economy of movement that already seemed typical of him and headed back the way he had come.

Nat raised an eyebrow at her dramatic statement. 'You would have been OK as long as you stayed with the car,' he pointed out. 'The Grangers would have come to look for you eventually.'

'Oh, I know. I wasn't worried about my safety.' The cab was blissfully cool after the crushing heat in the car.

Prue leant forward to adjust the vent so that the cold air blew directly onto her face. She had never understood the appeal of air-conditioning until she had come to Australia.

'You've saved me from having to explain what an idiot I've been,' she went on, sitting back with a sigh of relief. 'I was dreading it.'

'I can't see any of the Grangers getting angry with you,' said Nat in the calm way of a man who had no idea what it was like to do anything stupid or be afraid of anything.

'I know. That's what makes it worse!' sighed Prue. 'They're so nice and kind,' she tried to explain, seeing Nat's baffled look. 'They've been wonderful to me. I'd always wanted to work on a real outback cattle station, and getting a job at Cowen Creek was like a dream come true. Mr and Mrs Granger are great—and Ross, of course.'

She had meant it to sound like a casual aside, but her voice came out ridiculously strangled instead. It was hopeless, thought Prue in despair. All she had to do was *think* about Ross and her heart clenched, squeezing the air from her lungs. She couldn't even say his name without her throat thickening.

She coughed slightly to clear it. 'Well, anyway, I just love being at Cowen Creek,' she went on, 'but I'm sure they must think I'm really stupid. They're just too polite to say so.'

Nat glanced at her. She was staring disconsolately through the windscreen, her unruly hair pushed behind her ears to reveal a fine-boned profile. He didn't think she looked stupid. Her face was warm, alert, quirky in an attractive way, but not stupid.

'Why should they think that?' he asked.

'Because I am,' said Prue glumly. 'I can't seem to do anything right. I fainted dead away once when I cut myself with a knife, and I couldn't even *watch* when they were dehorning the calves. And then the other day I nearly had a fit when I found a snake in the onion sack— they all thought that was *really* funny,' she remembered with a sigh. 'They said it wasn't poisonous but I didn't know that, did I?' she added, turning to Nat almost belligerently, as if he had been the one who had laughed at the sight of her screaming blue murder in the storeroom.

'There's no reason why you should,' he agreed gravely, and Prue subsided a little.

'I'd love to be able to ride well,' she went on, 'but all their horses seem to be half wild, and I keep falling off.' Her cheeks burned with humiliation as she remembered how Ross had grinned as he picked her up. 'I just seem to be hopeless at everything.'

'Except cooking,' Nat pointed out. 'Bill Granger told me you're the best cook they've ever had.'

'Anyone can cook,' said Prue dismissively. 'I want to be able to do the things everyone else can do out here.'

'Like what?'

'Like lasso a calf. Like mend a fence or fix a water pipe. Like brand a cow without passing out. Like remembering to check the fuel before setting out to drive to town!' She folded the shopping list sadly in her lap, turning it over and over until it was no more than a tiny square. 'I'm a liability the moment I step outside the homestead!'

'You're just getting used to a different way of doing things,' said Nat, but Prue refused to be consoled.

'I've already been here three months,' she grumbled. 'How much longer is it going to take?'

'Why does it matter?' he asked. 'You can't help what you are.'

'But that's just it! I don't want to be like me! I was born and brought up in London, but that doesn't mean I'm condemned to be a city girl my whole life, does it? I don't want people to think of me as a prissy Pom mincing around the outback, no good for anything except peeling a few potatoes or making a cake. I want to be...'

The kind of girl Ross would fall in love with. The kind of girl he would marry.

She could hardly tell Nat Masterman *that*, though, could she?

'...I want to *belong*,' she finished instead. She turned to Nat, and he was very aware of the intense, silver-grey gaze on his face. 'Do you think that's possible?'

Nat kept his eyes firmly on the track ahead. 'Why not?'

'Ross doesn't think it is.' Prue dropped her eyes and concentrated on unfolding the shopping list. 'He thinks you have to be born here to belong. I've been trying so hard to prove him wrong, and now I've gone and made a fool of myself all over again by forgetting to check the fuel in the car! If you hadn't come along, it would have looked as if I couldn't even manage to go into town and pick up a few groceries without them having to come out and rescue me. I know they wouldn't have been angry, but they're all so busy at the moment and it would have been a real nuisance...'

She trailed off, imagining the scene if Ross or one of the stockmen had been sent out to find her, and her eyes lifted to Nat's calm profile once more. 'That's why I said you'd saved my life,' she told him.

'You know, you're worried about nothing,' said Nat. 'The Grangers like you. They've told me so, and they're not the kind of people who pretend. You're fun for them to have around and, more importantly, you're a good cook. They've got stockmen to help them outside. What they really want is someone to produce meals for every-one on time, and you can do that. If they don't want you to be different, why should you?'

'Because Ross wants me to be different.' The words were out before Prue could stop them and she bit her lip, turning her head away and letting her hair swing forward so that when Nat glanced at her he could see only the curve of her jaw and the long line of her throat.

'Are you sure about that?' he asked dryly after a mo-ment. 'When I saw the two of you together at Ellie Walker's wedding, it looked as if he liked you just the way you were.'

Surprise brought Prue's head round. 'You were at the wedding?' She frowned slightly. 'I didn't notice you.'

There had been no reason for her to have noticed him, Nat thought without resentment. He didn't have Ross Granger's famous looks or charm. He had only noticed her because of the way her eyes had shone that night. It was as if a light had been switched on inside her. She'd seemed to be literally glowing with happiness. Nat re-membered wondering what it would be like to have a girl look at him the way Prue had looked at Ross.

'I got the impression you didn't notice anyone except Ross,' he said with a wry sideways look.

It was true. Prue had had eyes only for Ross that night. The other guests, even the bride and groom, had been no more than a background blur to the wonderful, glorious fact that she was with him. It had been a perfect evening. Ross had ignored all the other girls there. He had flirted only with her, danced only with her, and then he had driven her back to Cowen Creek and kissed her in the car outside the homestead.

Prue had been so certain that that night was to prove
the beginning of the rest of her life. Ross was everything
she'd ever wanted, and for a while she had floated dreamily through the days, imagining how happy they would
be together, writing home to tell her family that she had
at last found the love of her life.

And she had. It was just that Ross didn't seem to think
that he had found *his*.

She smoothed the shopping list in her lap. 'I'm in love
with Ross,' she said in a low voice, unable to resist the
urge to talk about him, not quite sure why she had chosen
Nat to confide in other than the fact that he seemed so
solid and dependable. There was something steady about
him, something strong and sure about his hands on the
steering wheel.

She had been longing for someone to talk to. The only
other woman at Cowen Creek was Ross's mother, who
was very kind but not the sort you could pour your heart
out to, and although the jackaroos were more or less her
own age, Prue's mind boggled at the idea of trying to
discuss emotions with them. Nat might not be the ideal
confidant, but he wouldn't sigh or sneer or roll his eyes
the way the others would. And he wouldn't gossip. You
could tell just by looking at him that gossip, like haste,
was an alien concept.

'I've never felt like this about anyone before,' she went
on without looking at him, and now that she had started
talking she couldn't stop. 'I fell in love with him the
moment I saw him, just like in all the books. He was
waiting to pick me up when I got off the bus from Alice
Springs, and that was it. He's like a dream come true.'

Prue looked out at the heat shimmering over the salt-
bush, but she was seeing Ross as he had been that day,

with his dancing blue eyes and his devastating smile and that body...

She swallowed at the very thought of him. 'It's not just the way he looks,' she said. 'He's funny and he's charming, but he's down to earth at the same time...oh, I can't explain,' she confessed helplessly, the tumbling words slowing at last. 'He's just...the only man I'll ever want.'

Nat's gaze flickered to Prue's face and then back to the track. What *was* it about Ross? he wondered. He was a good-looking bloke, of course, but there must be something else to reduce a girl like Prue to this kind of state. She was obviously besotted, the way every other girl in the district under the age of thirty seemed to have been besotted with him at one stage or another.

'What's the problem?' he asked.

Prue was taken aback by the sudden question. Thinking about Ross, she had almost forgotten that she was talking to Nat. 'Problem?'

'I guess you wouldn't be telling me this if Ross felt the same way.'

'No.' Her shoulders slumped and she sighed. 'He likes me, I suppose, but he doesn't love me. As far as Ross is concerned, our relationship will only last as long as my visa. The Grangers get a girl in to cook during the dry season every year, and Ross probably flirts with all of them.' It was hard to keep the bitterness out of her voice. 'I'm just the current model.'

Knowing Ross, and the succession of girls who had worked at Cowen Creek, Nat thought it was more than likely, but he didn't think that Prue would want to hear that.

'Ross is all right,' he said uncomfortably. 'He's just young.'

'He's twenty-seven, two years older than me. It's not that young.'

'It's not that old either. There's plenty of time before Ross needs to think about settling down.'

'And when he does, he's going to pick a good outback girl who'll make him a practical wife,' said Prue miserably.

Nat thought that was more than likely, too. For all his charm of manner, Ross had always struck him as having a hard head on his shoulders. 'Is that what he says?' he asked, deciding to stay neutral.

'He doesn't have to.' She looked down at her hands. 'He's made it very clear that he doesn't think I can cope with life on a station like Cowen Creek. I'm just someone else he can have a good time with, not someone he would ever think about spending his life with.'

Her voice wobbled slightly, but she was determined not to give in to tears the way she had done when the car had first spluttered to a halt and left her stranded with only the thought of how much her stupidity just seemed to prove Ross's point. She stiffened her lip. 'I don't belong,' she finished bleakly, 'and Ross thinks I never will.'

'You can't blame him for thinking about how you would manage,' said Nat cautiously. He had the nasty feeling that he was getting out of his depth. 'It's a hard life out here, if you're not used to it.'

'All I want is the chance to *get* used to it,' said Prue with another sigh.

To Nat's relief, they were approaching the turn-off onto the sealed road, where the track was marked by an old tractor tyre on which 'Cowen Creek' had been painted. He changed gear, wishing that it were as easy to disengage a conversation.

'There's no reason why you shouldn't,' he said as he

looked up and down the long, straight, empty stretch of road before pulling out. 'By the end of the season you'll be carrying on like you were born here, and who's to say Ross won't change his mind? You just need to give him time.'

'But I haven't got time,' Prue protested. 'That's just it. I've got to go home in three weeks.'

He shot her a look of surprise. 'Has your visa run out already?'

'No, my sister's getting married.' Prue's tone didn't suggest she found it much cause for celebration. 'Originally they were going to have an autumn wedding, but then Cleo decided it would be much nicer for everyone if they had it in summer instead, so I've got to cut short my trip. I promised I'd be there, and I can't let her down.'

She stared disconsolately out of the window, imagining London with its grey streets and its grey buildings and its grey clouds. Here the sky was an intense, glaring blue and the air was diamond-bright and the heat shimmered over the red earth and wavered along the vast, distant horizon. And somewhere out there Ross was riding his horse, sitting easily in the saddle, smiling that smile of his...

'I wish I could stay,' she sighed. 'It's not just because of Ross. I love it here. I suppose I always had a pretty romantic idea of the outback, and I didn't really know what to expect. When I heard about the job at Cowen Creek I was half afraid that I would be disappointed, but the moment I arrived I fell in love with the place.

'It was like coming home,' she said slowly, the grey eyes dreamy and unfocused as she remembered how she had felt. 'It was as if I'd always known the light and the stillness and the silence. I love the birds and the trees along the creeks, and the way the screen door bangs.'

She glanced at Nat, half-defiant, half shame-faced. 'That's why it bothers me so much that I don't belong, why I wish so much that I could. Does that sound stupid?'

'No, it doesn't sound stupid.' He turned his head and smiled at her, a warm smile that illuminated his quiet face and left Prue oddly startled, even breathless, at the transformation.

'It doesn't sound stupid at all,' he said again. 'That's the way I feel about the outback, too.'

'Really?'

Slewing round as far as she could in her seat-belt, Prue studied Nat with new interest. She had never taken much notice of him before, beyond registering his air of unhurried calm, but now she looked at him properly and was surprised at what she saw.

It wasn't that he was handsome, at least not in the way Ross was handsome. His hair was an indeterminate shade of brown, his eyes were brown—in fact, everything about him seemed to be brown. Brown skin, brown watch, strong brown hands on the wheel. He was even wearing a brown shirt.

But still, there was *something* about him. It was more to do with his air of quiet self-assurance than any particular arrangement of his features, Prue decided. If he wasn't so understated, he might even be quite attractive. His colouring might not be very obvious, but there was nothing indeterminate about that lean jaw, or the angles of his face, or the cool, firm mouth that had smiled with such astonishing effect.

Prue's eyes rested on it speculatively. It was a pity Nat didn't smile more often, she thought, remembering how white his teeth were, the way his eyes had crinkled at the corners and the creases had deepened in his cheeks, and for some reason a tiny, almost imperceptible tingle tip-toed down her spine and made her shiver.

Puzzled by her silence, Nat looked across to check that she was all right and their eyes met for a brief instant. There was nothing in his expression to suggest that he was aware of how closely she had been studying him, but Prue felt a blush steal up her cheeks and she jerked her gaze away.

'You're lucky,' she muttered, averting her face and conscious of a quite inexplicable feeling of shyness. 'You belong here. You don't have to go to London and wonder if you'll ever see the outback again.'

Nat didn't answer immediately. A road train was bearing down on them, and he lifted a hand to acknowledge the driver's wave as it thundered past with four long trailers.

'You'll just have to come back after the wedding,' he said when it had gone, able to put his foot down on the accelerator at last. 'The Grangers will still be here, and I'm sure they'd give you another job.'

'I'm not sure I'll be able to do that.' Prue had recovered from her momentary confusion. 'It took me ages to save the money for this trip, and I've spent it all now. If I wanted to buy another ticket, I'd have to start all over again.'

'Couldn't you do that?'

'I could, but by the time I'd got enough money together I'd probably be too old to get a work permit—and even if I wasn't, they would have had to have found a new cook for Cowen Creek.'

What was the betting that the next cook would be young, and pretty, and completely at home in the outback? Just the type to convince Ross that it was time to settle down, in fact. Desperation clutched at Prue's heart as she imagined coming back to find that Ross had given up waiting for her to get used to the bush and married someone much more suitable instead.

'So what you need,' said Nat, following his own train of thought, 'is a short-term job that will pay you enough to cover your fare back to Australia?'

Prue nodded. 'Except I'll probably need at least two jobs in order to save anything. I could get some office work during the day and waitress in the evenings, and if I stay with my parents I won't have to pay London rents, which would make a difference. It'll be all right if it's not for too long,' she tried to convince herself.

It would still take months before she could get back to Australia, she calculated in despair, and she sighed. 'Perhaps I could rob a bank or something!'

'What about a job that paid your flight back to Australia instead?'

'I can't see there being many of *those* advertised in the jobs pages,' said Prue glumly. 'Robbing a bank would be easier than finding a job like that. I might as well think about sprouting wings and flying back myself!'

'You shouldn't be so negative,' said Nat. 'Do you know anything about babies?'

Prue was momentarily thrown by the sudden change of subject. 'Babies?' she echoed uncertainly. 'As in very small people, dirty nappies and sleepless nights?'

Nat grimaced. 'It sounds as if you *do* know about them,' he said in a dry voice.

'I spent a lot of time with my elder sister's children when they were tiny. I've always loved babies,' she told him. 'They're a lot of work, but they're so gorgeous and…'

She broke off, belatedly realising why he might be asking and sat bolt upright to turn to him, her face suddenly alight with excitement. 'You don't know anyone who wants a nanny, do you?'

'Yes,' said Nat, nodding and the corner of his mouth lifted in a slight smile. '*I* do.'

CHAPTER TWO

PRUE'S grey eyes widened. 'You've got children?'

There was no reason why he shouldn't, of course, but she couldn't help feeling surprised. He seemed so self-contained that it was hard to imagine him with a wife amid the cheerful chaos of family life.

What would Nat's wife be like? Prue wondered. Probably as cool and sensible as he was himself. Certainly not the kind of woman who would forget to put fuel in the car, or cry, or pour out her heart to a virtual stranger, she decided, and felt unaccountably depressed.

'I'm going to have two.' Nat's smile was a little twisted as he thought about how much his life was going to change.

'Going to...?'

Glancing sideways, Nat caught her puzzled expression. 'They're not mine,' he explained. 'I'm talking about my brother's children, William and Daisy. They're twins, just eight months old and I'm their guardian now.' He paused. 'Ed and his wife were killed in a car accident in England a couple of months ago.'

Shocked, Prue pressed her hand to her mouth. 'How terrible,' she said, conscious of how inadequate her words sounded.

'I thought you might have heard about the accident,' said Nat after a moment. 'The Grangers knew Ed and Laura pretty well. They bought a property just to the east

of Cowen Creek last year, and they'd help each other out
on big musters sometimes.'

Prue shook her head. 'I didn't know,' she said. She
had been too wrapped up in Ross to take any interest in
the Grangers' neighbours she realised, ashamed. 'I'm so
sorry,' she went on, biting her lip. 'What were they doing
in England?'

'Laura was English, like you. Ed met her when he was
over in London, but they married out here. Laura loved
the outback, too, and she was quite happy to live here
but she felt guilty about her parents. They're quite el-
derly, and couldn't manage the trip out to Australia, so
they hadn't been at the wedding. When the twins were
born, she knew they would be longing to see their grand-
children and Ed promised that he would take her and the
babies to London for a visit instead.

'That was in April,' Nat went on. 'It's a busy time of
year, but Ed knew how much it would mean to Laura,
so he asked me to keep an eye on things while he was
gone. He said they would only be a month.'

The careful lack of expression in his voice made Prue's
heart twist with pity, and she cringed as she remembered
how she had whinged on about her own problems which
were so pathetic in comparison to his.

'What happened?' she asked awkwardly.

'They'd been in London three weeks when Laura's
parents offered to look after the twins for a day so that
she and Ed could have some time to themselves. It was
the first time they'd left William and Daisy. Apparently
it was a nice day, and they decided to drive out to the
country…'

He trailed off, and Prue found herself imagining Ed
and Laura kissing the babies goodbye, waving cheerfully
as they got into the car and drove off, looking forward

to a day together alone away from the city's noise and grime. Not knowing that they would never be coming back.

'They were in a head-on collision with a van,' Nat finished. 'The police told us that they would have both been killed instantly.'

'But the babies weren't with them?'

'No, they were with Laura's parents so they're fine.' As fine as they could be when their world had been torn apart, Nat amended grimly to himself.

He was very grateful to Prue for not offering false comfort or asking him how he had felt, what he was still feeling. He didn't want to talk about that.

'Where are they now?' asked Prue, almost as if she understood intuitively that he was happier sticking to the practicalities of the situation he had to deal with now.

'They're still with Laura's parents in London,' he said. 'I went over as soon as I heard. Ed and Laura wanted William and Daisy to grow up as Australians, and they knew that her parents would be in no position to look after them, so they'd made a will appointing me as guardian. I don't think they thought for a minute that anything would ever happen to them, that I would ever need to take responsibility for their children.'

'But now that's what you've got to do?'

'Yes.' His glance flickered over to Prue. She had turned slightly in her seat to face him as far as she could in the confines of her seatbelt, her expression warm and sympathetic. 'There was no way I could bring William and Daisy back with me after the funeral,' he told her, and he found himself hoping that she would understand and approve of what he had done. 'I arranged for a nanny to look after them with the Ashcrofts—Laura's parents—until I could sort things out here and make sure that I

would be able to care for them properly, but I think it's
important for me to go and get them as soon as possible.'

Prue nodded understandingly. 'The longer you leave
them, the more attached they will become to the nanny
and the harder it will be to take them away.'

'Exactly.' Nat looked at her gratefully. 'The trouble is,
I'm going to need help. I don't know anything about
babies. I'm not sure I would be able to cope with one
baby on a plane, let alone two. That's where you come
in,' he said. 'I think we may be able to help each other.
You want to come back to Australia; I want someone to
help me look after William and Daisy. I'll buy you a
return ticket if you'll fly back with me and the twins,' he
finished.

For a moment, Prue could only stare at him, unable to
believe that he could sound so casual. 'That's...
incredibly generous,' she stammered, not entirely
convinced that he knew what a generous offer it was.

'Not if you think about how much I need you,' said
Nat with a wry glance. 'I can put a mob of cattle through
the yards, and do all those things that you said you
wanted to be able to do earlier, but I don't know where
to begin with a baby! If you come, you're going to have
to teach me how to feed them and change them and bath
them and do all the other things they need. Could you
do that?'

'Well, yes, I suppose so, but—'

'It's not just a question of the flight either. Eve, the
nanny who's looking after William and Daisy at the moment, thinks that it would be upsetting for them to be
suddenly taken away from everything that's familiar.
They won't remember Australia now. She suggested that
I spend a few weeks getting to know them before bring-

ing them back, and it would make sense for you to come along too.'

'I can see that,' said Prue, nodding. 'They would need to get used to being with us.'

'And then there's the Ashcrofts,' said Nat. 'They were too distressed to talk much when I was there for the funeral, but they'll probably want to see who's going to be bringing their grandchildren up.'

'How do they feel about you taking William and Daisy away?' Prue tried to imagine her own parents in a similar situation. 'Don't they mind?' she asked curiously.

Nat thought about it. 'I think they know they can't manage the twins on their own,' he said at length. 'Losing Laura was a terrible blow for them—she was their only child—and it's hard enough for them to cope as it is, without the worry of bringing up children. That doesn't mean they're not concerned, of course,' he added, noting with one part of his mind a plane's wing glinting in the sun as it turned. The airport was just ahead, which meant that it wasn't far to Mathison, and he wanted Prue to understand the situation before they got there.

'They've never been to Australia, and the outback sounds a very strange place to them. They were worried about the fact that William and Daisy will be isolated, and that as a bachelor I wouldn't be able to look after them properly, but they were all right when I told them that I was engaged, and that the twins would grow up in a family. I said that the next time I came I'd bring my fiancée with me so that they could meet her too.'

There was a pause. 'I didn't know you were engaged,' said Prue after a moment, and wondered why her voice sounded so hollow all of a sudden.

Or why she was even surprised.

There was no reason why Nat shouldn't be engaged,

just as there had been no reason why he shouldn't have a wife and children. It was just that, having established that he *wasn't* married, she had somehow assumed that he never would be. And if he had a fiancée, why did he need *her* to help him with William and Daisy?

'I was then,' said Nat, answering one of her unspoken questions as she stole a puzzled look at him. His voice had no inflexion whatsoever and it was impossible to tell how he felt about the fact that his engagement apparently belonged to the past.

'I'm not any more,' he added when Prue continued to look blank.

In one way, it made it easier for Nat that she knew nothing about Kathryn, but a perverse part of him couldn't help wishing that she hadn't made it quite so obvious that she had never taken the slightest interest in him. He was surprised that she had even known his name.

'You obviously didn't know that either,' he commented dryly.

'No.' Prue shook her head. 'The Grangers don't go in much for gossip,' she said. 'I'm sorry,' she added, and then realised that she sounded as if she regretted not knowing about the break-up of his engagement. 'I mean, I'm sorry about your engagement.'

'Don't be,' said Nat. They were driving past the airport now, where he had said goodbye to Kathryn before she'd got on the plane back to Perth. He remembered the softness of her kiss, the swing of her hair as she'd turned, the unmistakable relief in the way she'd walked away.

'It was a mutual decision,' he told Prue. 'Kathryn and I have known each other a long time. She's got a good job in Perth, and we'd deliberately decided on a long engagement so that she could concentrate on a big project she's working on at the moment. When I got back from

London I realised that it wasn't fair to ask her to give everything up to look after two small children, so we talked about it and agreed to…postpone…the idea of marriage for the time being. It's better this way for both of us.'

He didn't sound bitter, but Prue had the impression that he was picking his words carefully, editing as he went along. He could say what he liked about it being a mutual decision, but he was obviously still besotted by her, she decided, unsure why she felt slightly peeved at the idea. Why else would make excuses for her?

She found herself disliking the unknown Kathryn intensely, and feeling obscurely cross with Nat at the same time. He *ought* to mind that his fiancée had chosen her job over him.

'It's not really better for you, though, is it?' she said, more sharply than she had intended. 'How are you going to look after the twins on your own?'

If Nat was surprised at her tone, he didn't show it. 'I'll have to hire a nanny,' he said. 'I asked Eve if she would think about coming out to Australia with William and Daisy, even if only for the first few weeks, but I've just had a letter from her saying that she's getting married and doesn't want to leave England.'

Prue couldn't imagine anyone turning down the chance to travel to Australia, marriage or no marriage. Ahead, the heat beat down on the road, creating a wavering mirage that blurred the horizon between the crushing blue sky and the sparse scrub that stretched off as far as the eye could see and beyond. It was like being in a different dimension altogether—so much space and so much light that Prue would sometimes feel dizzy and disembodied.

How could anyone *not* want to be here? Prue shook her head pityingly.

She brought her attention back to Nat, who was talking about the arrangements he would have to make. 'I've contacted a couple of agencies here to see if anyone would be prepared to travel to London with me and help bring William and Daisy back. Ideally, it would be someone who wanted to stay at Mack River on a permanent basis, but they haven't come up with anyone yet. That's why I thought of you,' he said, glancing at Prue. 'When you said how much you wanted to come back to Australia, it seemed you could be just the person I need. I know you wouldn't want to stay permanently, but it might take me some time to find someone suitable. You could stay at Mack River while you looked for another job in the area, if that's what you want. You'd only be gone about a month. The Grangers might even keep your job open for you.'

Prue sat up straighter, fired up by the mere possibility. 'I could ask them,' she agreed excitedly. 'They'll need to replace me while I'm away, but maybe they'll get someone who doesn't want to stay.'

'More than likely,' said Nat. 'There's always a high turnover of staff during the dry season. It's too hot, or too isolated, or too boring, or too much like hard work.

'There aren't many people like you,' he told Prue with a slight smile, and she found herself wishing that he'd smile the way he had smiled before.

It wouldn't take much, just a deepening of the creases on either side of his mouth, just a parting of the lips, just a crinkling of his eyes. She remembered how startled she had been, the way her heart had jolted, that odd sensation of suddenly finding herself face to face with a stranger.

For some reason, Prue's cheeks were tingling, and when she put up a hand to feel her skin she realised that she was actually blushing! Embarrassed, without knowing why, she dragged her eyes away from Nat's mouth, which had lifted into something that was almost—but not quite—a proper smile, and forced her mind back to what they had been talking about.

For a terrible moment her mind was blank, before memory kicked in. Going back to Cowen Creek...how could she possibly have forgotten?

Giving herself a mental shake, Prue let herself picture the situation. If she went back, Ross would know that she was serious about wanting to live in the outback. He would realise that she meant what she said, and wasn't just amusing herself for a few months, the way the girls who saw a stint on a cattle station as part of travelling around Australia did.

Nat's offer would mean that she would only be gone for a month or so. Surely even Ross couldn't forget her in that time? He might even miss her. The thought flickered into life, grew stronger. Didn't they say that absence made the heart grow fonder?

Prue slid a sideways glance at Nat from under her lashes. He was a bit older, of course, and not in Ross's league when it came to looks, but he wasn't *un*attractive. What would Ross think when he found out that she was going to spend a month with Nat? Might he even be jealous? Prue wondered hopefully.

Remembering how miserable she had been less than an hour ago, Prue smiled to herself. 'I'm beginning to think that forgetting to check the fuel today was the best thing that ever happened to me,' she said slowly.

'Does that mean you'll take the job?'

'I'd love it,' said Prue honestly, 'but...well, I don't have *that* much experience of babies. Wouldn't you rather have someone more qualified?' She grimaced, thinking of the catalogue of stupid mistakes she had made just since she had been at Cowen Creek, let alone the rest of her life. 'Someone more efficient?'

Nat took his eyes off the road for a moment to look at her, with her unruly curls and her wide, tilting mouth and the nose that was just a little too big. 'I'd rather have someone like you,' he said.

He didn't know how to explain that there was a warmth about her that was much more appealing than efficiency. He might not be able to imagine her keeping an immaculately tidy house, but he could picture her holding a baby in her arms, offering unlimited tenderness and security and love.

A little too vividly, in fact.

Nat frowned and concentrated on his driving once more. 'You're a nice girl,' he said gruffly. 'The Grangers like you. You love the outback and you want to come back. Those are all good enough reasons as far as I'm concerned. And then, you need to go to London just when I do...'

'You could almost say that we're meant for each other!' Prue finished for him cheerfully.

A tiny pause.

We're meant for each other. Her words echoed in the silence between them, and she suddenly realised how easily Nat might have misinterpreted them.

'I mean...job-wise,' she added uncomfortably.

Nat flashed her an enigmatic look. 'What else?' he said in a dry voice.

Nobody could say that Mathison was a pretty town, but Prue loved the old hotel, with its wide, wooden verandahs, the great iron water-tanks beside every house, and the pokey general store which had a weird and wonderful selection of goods and an eccentric taste in displays. Prue perked up as they drove along the wide street.

She had hated the thought that she might never see it again, of returning to soulless supermarkets where everything was wrapped in layers of plastic.

Now, thanks to Nat, she could stop worrying about whether every trip would be her last and just enjoy being here. Oh, and do the shopping, of course.

Nat dropped her at the store while he went off to find some fuel. Prue still had her list, although it was so creased from being folded and unfolded so much that she could hardly read it. It was better than nothing, though. Wandering around the store, Prue found it harder to concentrate on the shopping than she would have thought. She had to keep stopping and peering at the tattered piece of paper, while her mind drifted back to Nat and the fantastic offer that he had made.

The more Prue thought about it, the better it seemed. There was no way she could miss Cleo's wedding, but it had been hard not to resent the fact that she would have to leave Australia much earlier than she had originally intended. Now she would not only be a good sister, but she should also be able to spend another whole year here, and who knew what could happen in that time?

Prue could hardly believe her luck. Her momentary embarrassment had passed, and now all she could think about was how everything was turning out better than she would have believed possible. No wonder it was hard to concentrate on how much flour and sugar she needed!

She was coming back. Prue hugged the knowledge to her. Coming back to this place she loved so much.

And to Ross.

Prue's heart melted when she thought about the daredevil blue of his eyes, about the way he threw his head back when he laughed and the air of suppressed energy he carried around with him, and happiness bubbled along her veins. Surely meeting Nat meant that she and Ross were destined for each other after all?

When Nat found her, Prue was gazing at a pyramid of tinned vegetables, her mouth curved in a dreamy smile. Her sunglasses were pushed on top of her head, drawing the tousled hair away from her face, and even in the dim old-fashioned light of the store Nat could see that her grey eyes were shining.

There had been a moment in the ute when something had tightened in the air between them, but whatever it had been it had gone now. Nat could tell just by the way Prue smiled when she saw him, a wide, open smile that said more clearly than words ever could that she might think of him as a friend, or an employer, but certainly not as a man.

Which was just as well, in the circumstances, Nat told himself.

'You look happy,' he said.

'I am.' Prue beamed at him. 'I was just standing here, thinking about how miserable I was when I set out this afternoon. I was convinced that I would never have a chance to persuade Ross to love me, that I'd have to go home and never see him again. When that car ran out of fuel. I just sat there and bawled my eyes out,' she confessed. 'I was really pathetic! And then—' she spread her hands '—you came along and suddenly everything is possible again.'

She looked at Nat with her frank eyes. 'I feel as if today is going to prove to be the turning point of my whole life,' she told him, 'and it's all thanks to you.'

Her face was alight with happiness, and Nat was suddenly aware of how close she was standing. She was so warm, he thought, so vibrant, so open and uncomplicated.

So in love with Ross Granger.

He stepped away from her, unsettled to realise that he didn't want her thanks. 'Are you ready?' he asked curtly.

'Yes, the boxes are by the door.'

Prue was puzzled and a little hurt by his brusqueness as they carried the boxes of groceries out to the ute. The light hit her like a blow as she stepped out of the shade of the verandah, and she couldn't wait to hand over her box so that she could pull her sunglasses back down onto her nose.

Nat didn't seem to notice at all. None of the men she had met wore sunglasses, relying on their hats to protect them from the glare instead, she supposed, but the corners of their eyes were always creased from years of squinting into the sun. Prue could see the fan of lines at the edge of Nat's eyes now as he loaded the boxes into the back of the ute and covered them with a tarpaulin to keep out the dust.

Looking at those lines gave her a funny feeling inside—either that, or the sun was getting to her—and her gaze dropped to his mouth, which was set in a bleak line that made her frown slightly.

His expression was closed, shuttered even. Of course, Nat would be an unemotional man at the best of times, but he hadn't been like this when they drove in together. She remembered how he had smiled, the look in his eyes when he had said, 'I want someone like you.'

It was as if he had withdrawn into himself since then. As if, Prue thought slowly, her bubbling enthusiasm had made him retreat behind a barrier of impenetrable reserve. As if he didn't like her being happy.

And why should he?

Prue felt a sickening wave of shame roll over her. She had forgotten what the trip to London was going to mean for Nat. For her, the job he had offered her meant the possibility of romance, a chance to achieve her heart's desire. For him, it meant only the aftermath of tragedy.

'I'm sorry,' she said in a small voice as she got into the ute beside him.

Nat was bending to push the key into the ignition, but at her apology he straightened in surprise. 'Sorry?' he echoed blankly. 'What for?'

'I must sound absolutely heartless, wittering on about Ross and coming back to Australia when all you're thinking about is your brother.' Prue pulled the seatbelt around her and fastened it into place before turning contritely to Nat. 'It's going to be a terrible trip for you, I can see that. I wish you'd just told me to shut up,' she said in a burst of honesty. 'I feel *awful* now!'

Nat's expression was rueful as he started the engine and pushed up the gearstick on the steering column. He hadn't been thinking about Ed at all, he thought wryly. He had been thinking about her.

'You mustn't think like that,' he said, contrite in his turn. 'It's the last thing Ed would have wanted, or Laura either come to that. They were both real live-wires, and they believed in deciding what you want and going for it.

'They'd approve of you doing whatever you could to get back to Ross,' he told Prue. 'You don't need to feel guilty about being happy over the fact that I need you to help me with William and Daisy. Ed would be the first person cheering you on!'

His voice was warm when he talked about his brother. 'You must miss him,' said Prue quietly.

Nat hesitated. He wasn't used to discussing his feelings, but somehow it was easy to talk to Prue.

'Yes,' he admitted. 'I do. I miss him a lot. Ed was only a couple of years younger than me, and there were just the two of us when we were growing up. We ran Mack River together when our parents died, and then Ed met Laura, and they bought their own property. I'd got used to them not being around every day, but still…it's hard sometimes to believe I won't see him again.'

He wasn't looking at Prue, but she felt her throat tighten. 'I'm sorry,' she said again, knowing that it was inadequate, but knowing too that there was nothing else to say.

Nat's smile was rather twisted. 'I'm sorry too,' he said slowly, 'but it's William and Daisy who matter now. I've got to think about them, not Ed, and that's what I'm going to do.'

When they got back to Prue's car, they transferred the groceries into the back, and then Nat took the can of fuel he had bought and poured it carefully into the tank. He had brushed aside Prue's attempts to pay and she watched him, feeling helpless and more than a little disconcerted to discover how easy it was to accept being looked after by someone so competent.

It was difficult to imagine that barely two hours ago she had had trouble remembering his name. Already there was something very familiar about him. How much more familiar would he be after they'd spent almost a month together in London?

The thought was vaguely disconcerting, and Prue frowned. It wasn't as if they were going to be intimate, she reassured herself. It was just a job like any other. And Nat was hardly likely to show any interest in *her*, was he?

Even if she hadn't been in love with Ross, she would have little to appeal to a man like Nat. He was quite a bit older than her, for a start, and to him she probably seemed very young and very silly. Correction, thought

Prue, cringing inwardly as she remembered some of the things she had said: she must *definitely* seem very young and very silly.

Anyway, Nat himself had sounded far from over his broken engagement. Prue couldn't help wondering what Kathryn was like. What kind of woman could break through that quiet self-containment and unlock his reserve? She must be quite special, Prue decided.

Hidden behind her sunglasses, her gaze rested on Nat as he tipped the can higher to let the last drops of diesel trickle into the tank and she tried to imagine him in love. He wasn't a demonstrative man, she guessed, but behind closed doors...well, that might be a different matter...

'OK, that's it.' Nat's voice broke into her thoughts as he dumped the empty can in the back of the ute. 'Start her up and we'll see if she goes now.'

Obediently, Prue climbed into the driver's seat and turned the key. The engine shuddered into life and then settled down to a steady tick.

'Do you ever get a day off?' Nat asked, laying a hand on the roof of the car and bending his head slightly so that he could talk to her through the open window.

'I don't do much on Sundays. Why?'

'We still need to sort out a few details about this trip,' he pointed out. 'I could fly over and pick you up next Sunday and you could spend the day at Mack Creek. It might not be a bad idea for you to see where the twins are going to grow up anyway, and we could talk about things then. It would give you a chance to think about what's involved too, and change your mind if you want to. How does that sound?'

'Fine,' said Prue. 'But aren't you coming to Cowen Creek now? I thought you wanted to see Bill Granger?'

'It can wait.' Nat didn't think he really wanted to go

to Cowen Creek now and watch Prue mooning over Ross. 'I think I'll get back.'

His face through the window was very close, and his features seemed uncannily clear and detailed. Prue felt as if she could see every crease at the corner of his eyes, every minute line texturing his skin, every hair that grew in the strong brown brows. She wanted to look away, but her gaze seemed to have snagged in his somehow.

'What shall I tell the Grangers?' she managed to ask.

'Just say that you met me in Mathison,' said Nat. 'There's no need to tell them about the fuel. You could say that we got talking and when I found out that you were going to London, I offered you the job. They know about Ed and Laura and the fact that I'm guardian to the twins now, so they probably won't even be surprised.'

'Right,' said Prue, finally succeeding in wrenching her eyes away. She put the car into gear and cleared her throat. 'I'll see you on Sunday, then.'

She had the impression that Nat was about to say something else, but in the end he just stepped back, slapping the car roof in a gesture of farewell.

'See you on Sunday,' was all he said.

CHAPTER THREE

IN THE event, it was Ross who flew Prue to Mack River the following Sunday.

'He was going to Mathison anyway,' Prue found herself explaining to Nat as together they watched Ross's Cessna speed down the airstrip and lift up into the blue. He dipped his wings in farewell and headed off in the direction of the town, leaving the two of them alone together in the crushing silence of the bush.

'It seemed silly for you to come all the way over to Cowen Creek when he could give me a lift here just as easily, but if you could fly me back that would be great.'

She could hear herself babbling, but she was unaccountably shy now that she was suddenly face to face with Nat again. She had forgotten how still he was, how quietly assured, how self-conscious he made her feel.

It was stupid to think that she needed to explain anything, anyway. Even if she hadn't already outlined the situation when she'd phoned to say that Ross would bring her over to Mack River, Nat hadn't said anything to indicate that he cared one way or another *how* she got there.

His greeting had been quite impersonal, as if she were no more than a temporary nanny he was employing to look after his small niece and nephew—which was all she was, of course. There had been no reason for Prue's heart to bump against her ribs when she caught sight of him through the plane window. He had been leaning against the ute in the shade, arms folded and long legs crossed at the ankle, his hat tilted down over his eyes as he waited for Ross to bring the plane to a halt.

He had straightened as she approached, pushing his hat back and smiling that slow smile that she remembered with such unnerving clarity, and for some reason Prue had burst into speech. Now, she made herself shut up.

'I thought you'd be glad of a chance to spend some time with Ross,' Nat commented, holding open the door of the ute for her.

'Yes,' said Prue, hearing the slight doubt in her voice too late. She *had* been glad, of course, but her pleasure in the flight had been rather spoiled by her nervousness at seeing Nat again and broaching the idea that had come to her as she had driven back to Cowen Creek that day.

Still, it had been a great flight. She thought about Ross, the magnetism of his presence, the flashing smile as they'd swooped down over the bush, his eyes as blue as the sky around them. Remembering, Prue felt better.

'It was wonderful,' she told Nat, as if he had doubted her.

He got in beside her and switched on the engine. 'How does Ross feel about you coming back?'

'I think he's pleased,' said Prue cautiously.

It was clear Ross had no intention of committing himself to anything, but she was sure that there had been a definite warming in his attitude towards her since she had told him about the job Nat had offered her.

Of course, it might be wishful thinking, Prue reminded herself. It might just be that Ross was relieved to hear that she was really going and was only being so nice because he knew that she wouldn't be around for much longer.

She wished that she could have said that he was jealous of her spending a month in Nat's company, but none of the Grangers seemed to think that there was any chance—any *danger*, Prue corrected herself hastily—of Nat treating her as anything other than a nanny. They were united in believing that Kathryn would marry him in the end and that temporary help with the children was all that Nat would need. It would certainly never occur to any of them that he could ever be interested in any other woman.

'Nat's a one-woman man,' Ross had explained. 'He's adored Kathryn ever since they were kids. Everyone knew they would end up together eventually.'

'What's she like?' Prue had been unable to resist asking.

'Kathryn? She's great. Beautiful girl.' Ross narrowed his eyes appreciatively. 'Red hair, green eyes, legs that go on for ever and a smile that makes the sun look dim! She's bright too. She's got some kind of fancy job down in Perth.'

Prue didn't think he had to sound quite so enthusiastic about her. 'If she's that amazing, what's she doing with Nat?' she asked a little too tartly. 'I'd have thought he'd have been too down-to-earth for someone like Kathryn.'

Ross shrugged, obviously not seeing anything odd in the relationship at all, and it was Joyce Granger who offered an answer when she was helping Prue to wash up.

'Nat's always been able to manage Kathryn,' she said shrewdly. 'He's the only one who could. She was a very headstrong girl, but so pretty that her parents spoilt her rotten and let her do whatever she wanted. I think she needs Nat to keep her in line.'

'But if she needs him so much, why would she break off their engagement?'

'Kathryn's used to Nat looking after *her*. I think she

lost her nerve at the thought that she was going to have
to take second place for a while and help him care for
Ed's children, but she'll be back when she gets used to
the idea,' Joyce added comfortably.

Prue scrubbed the bottom of a saucepan with unnecessary vigour. 'What if Nat won't take her back?'

'Oh, Nat will take her back all right.' Joyce finished
drying a plate and put it on top of the pile. 'He'll never
love anyone but Kathryn. Those two are meant for each
other.'

Prue was still thinking about this exchange now, as
Nat drove along the bumpy track from the airstrip to the
homestead. She slid a covert glance at him from under
her lashes and had to admit that he didn't look as if he
were broken-hearted. Joyce Granger must be right. If he
wasn't miserable, it was because he was quite confident
that Kathryn would come back to him.

Which meant that her idea wouldn't work.

It had come to her when Cleo's letter had arrived two
days ago, a flash of inspiration to solve her problem and
Nat's, but if he were expecting Kathryn back at any minute, it might not work after all.... Prue chewed the edge
of her thumb, considering. Perhaps it would be better to
stick to being a nanny, and not mention the matter to
Nat?

The homestead was a low, rambling house, sheltered
on all sides by deep verandahs. Having been in the outback long enough to appreciate how precious the sight
of water could be, Prue was disappointed to find that it
wasn't right by the river that gave the station its name,
but when she asked Nat why the homestead wasn't
closer, Nat only laughed.

'You don't want to be anywhere near the river when

it's in flood,' he said. 'My grandfather knew what he was doing when he built the house here.'

In spite of the lack of a river view, Prue thought it was a wonderful house, cool and shady inside and set in an oasis of green. Bougainvillea scrambled over the front verandah, and a cluster of palms at the back gave the place a tropical, almost exotic feel, although it was clearly a long time since anyone had made gardening a priority.

Lunch proved to be a barbecue with the stockmen, a polite but taciturn group of men who eyed Prue curiously. She could tell they didn't think much of her. Every time she opened her mouth, she sounded more brittle and English and out of place, and she was secretly relieved when they disappeared to their own quarters and left her alone with Nat.

She helped him clear away the lunch dishes, and then Nat sent her out to sit on the back verandah while he made some coffee. She sat, enjoying the green shade and imagining what a restful place to live Mack River must be, with its tangled garden and its worn wooden floors and its air of masculine, faintly shabby comfort.

The homestead at Cowen Creek was very busy and functional in comparison, Prue couldn't help thinking. Of course, Ross lived there, and it was exciting just to be in his orbit, but sometimes it was quite exhausting to spend your day on tenterhooks, never knowing if the sound of the screen door meant that he was going to suddenly appear and bracing yourself for the crashing disappointment when someone else appeared instead.

No, living with Ross couldn't be said to be restful. But Mack River...Prue ran her hands appreciatively along the arms of the old wicker chair and gazed out at the garden…this was nice. Cool and calm and comfortable. A bit like Nat himself, in fact.

She smiled at the thought, and Nat, carrying two mugs of coffee, paused just behind the screen door.

He could see her quite clearly through the fine mesh as she sat and gazed dreamily out at the garden, her mouth curved in a secretive smile. She was wearing jeans and a pale pink shirt, and her unruly brown curls were pushed anyhow behind her ears. Nat thought that she looked relaxed and happy and disturbingly at home on his verandah.

What was she smiling about so dreamily? Ross, no doubt. Nat remembered the proprietorial way Ross had helped Prue down from the plane, and thought that the Grangers' son was a lot keener than she had admitted. She was probably planning her return to Cowen Creek already, imagining the scene where Ross swept her into his arms and vowed never to let her go again.

Nat scowled, and then wondered what he was doing. He ought to be glad for Prue's sake that Ross was showing more interest in her. Ross was the only reason that she was prepared to go to London and help him bring William and Daisy home. She wasn't doing it for *him*, Nat reminded himself. It would be a mistake to forget that.

Abruptly, he kicked the screen door open and its hinges creaked in protest. The sound made Prue jump, and she turned to see Nat coming towards her with a mug in each hand. His expression was not grim exactly, but somehow remote, and Prue was conscious of a feeling of disappointment. She had thought they had been getting on quite well.

'This is lovely,' she said politely, gesturing at the garden. If they were going to spend a month together, she had better get used to filling the silence. 'I'd like to sit here for ever!'

The thought crossed Nat's mind that he wouldn't mind her staying there for ever either, but he quashed it firmly. She was just being polite. The only way she would ever want to stay at Mack River was if Ross could be there too.

'I'm glad you like it,' he said distantly, and handed her one of the mugs.

Deliberately choosing the chair separated from hers by a small table, he sat down and leant forward, resting his arms on his knees so that he could cradle his own mug between his hands.

Somewhat daunted, Prue sipped her coffee and sought around for something else to say. In the end, the best she could manage was to thank him for lunch.

At least she could see a gleam of amusement in Nat's eyes as he glanced across at her. 'I don't think it will have been up to your standards!' he said. 'I've got a married man working here, and his wife cooks for us during the week, but, like you, she has a day off on Sunday and we have to look out for ourselves. We're not very adventurous when it comes to food, as you probably gathered!'

'I enjoyed it,' said Prue honestly. 'It's a real treat to eat anything I haven't cooked myself now!'

'The Grangers are going to miss you.' Nat looked back at the palms and tried not to sound too interested. 'Are they keeping your job open for you?'

'No.' Prue shook her head. 'They said they were sorry, but I told them when I arrived that I'd have to go back to London, and they've already promised another English girl that she can come and cook. She's a friend of a friend, I think, and she's already made arrangements to travel up from Adelaide.'

Nat frowned slightly. 'Do you still want to come back to Australia, in that case?'

'I'd rather go back to Cowen Creek, of course, but if that's not possible…well, maybe I could find another job in the district. It might even be better if I *wasn't* at Cowen Creek,' she went on thoughtfully, almost as if she were talking to herself. 'It can be awkward with us both living in the same house with his parents, and if I was working somewhere else Ross might not feel the same kind of pressure.'

Nat found it hard to believe that Ross knew what pressure was, but there was no point in saying that to Prue. She was obviously still obsessed with him. 'I haven't found a suitable nanny yet,' he said out loud. 'I'll need help with William and Daisy when I get back here and you could stay on, if you liked. Just until you found something better,' he added quickly, in case Prue thought he *wanted* her to stay. 'It wouldn't be anything permanent.'

Obviously not, thought Prue. Why would he want a permanent nanny when he was counting on Kathryn to help him look after William and Daisy? They would be a proper family then, and they wouldn't want any English nannies hanging around, invading their privacy and envying them their comfortable old homestead and cool garden.

Still, if Nat wanted to place all his faith in a girl who had already let him down once, that was his problem. Prue sat up a little straighter in her chair and pushed her hair away from her face with unconscious defiance. All *she* wanted was to be near Ross, and Nat's offer would at least mean that she had somewhere to go when she got

back to Australia. She would find something more suitable later.

'That sounds great,' she said.

'Then, if we're agreed, I'll book the flights next week,'
said Nat. 'When is your sister's wedding?'

'August the twenty-first, but I should really be in
London a week before that. Cleo wants me to be a bridesmaid,' Prue remembered gloomily, 'and I suppose I'll
have to make sure the dress fits and all that kind of thing.'

'You don't sound as if you're looking forward to it
very much,' Nat commented drily. 'I thought women
liked weddings?'

'I don't mind them if they're small, and everybody
knows each other, but this isn't going to be like that. Cleo
is determined to have a traditional wedding with all the
trimmings. At least I'll have missed most of the run-up,'
she tried to console herself. 'Judging by their letters,
Mum and Cleo are totally obsessed with all the arrangements, and my elder sister will be in there too, and they'll
all be arguing!'

Prue sighed. It wasn't the main reason she was dreading Cleo's wedding now, but it was bad enough. She
sipped morosely at her coffee.

'Cleo and Alex are both super-successful, and all the
other guests will be like them. I'll just be Cleo's odd
sister who doesn't have a career or a mortgage, and no
one will know what to say to me!'

Nat couldn't help laughing at her glum expression.
'I'm sure it won't be that bad!'

There was that smile of his again. Prue blinked as her
heart gave an odd little somersault and landed with a thud
that left her with a strange, breathless feeling. She looked
away.

'Well, anyway,' she said, clearing her throat, 'I'll be

free to help you with William and Daisy any time after the twenty-first.'

'We might as well fly over to London together in that case,' said Nat, and Prue was obscurely grateful to him for sounding so practical. 'While you're getting ready for the wedding, I can spend some time with the Ashcrofts. There are several things I need to sort out with them before the twins can come back to Australia.'

It would be a pretty grim week for him, Prue guessed. She would much rather help him through it than listen to heated debates about who would be wearing what, and which kind of canapés to serve at the reception.

'Are you going to stay with the Ashcrofts?' she asked him, turning slightly in her chair to face him over the table. It was a shame that she could only look at him when they were talking about practical arrangements and she could be sure that he wasn't going to startle her with a smile.

'No.' Nat put his mug down on the table and leant back in his chair with a grimace at the thought of the trip ahead of him. 'They haven't got that big a house, and with the twins and a nanny living with them they haven't got any extra room. In any case, I think having me to stay on top of everything else they have to deal with would be too much for them.'

'What are you going to do, then? Stay in a hotel?'

'I thought I might rent an apartment nearby,' he said slowly. 'Somewhere I could take William and Daisy during the day, and where they could eventually spend the night so they get used to the idea of being with me—and you,' he added after a moment.

'Good idea.' Prue kept her voice even, although there was something about the idea of sharing a flat with Nat, of spending the night together, that sent a funny feeling tiptoeing down her spine. They wouldn't be sharing a room, and they would only be together because of the babies, but still, there would be something intimate about the situation, she thought.

Not that it appeared to bother Nat. 'You know London,' he said. 'Do you think I'd be able to find somewhere like that to rent for a month?'

'It would probably be very expensive.' Prue was quite proud of how brisk she sounded. 'Where exactly do the Ashcrofts live?'

'In Wimbledon. It's easy to remember because of the tennis.'

'That's not far from my parents,' she said thoughtfully, pleased to have something else apart from the prospect of meeting Nat in the middle of the night to consider. 'I'll ask them if they know of anywhere. You never know, someone might be going away for the summer holidays and let you have their house in exchange for watering the plants and feeding the cat. I'll ask them, if you like,' she offered.

Nat nodded his thanks. 'That would be good.' He rubbed a hand over his face in a weary gesture. 'It would be one less thing to worry about, if it works out.'

Fascinated, Prue watched his hand moving along his jaw, and was horrified to feel her own palms prickle, as if she could feel the male roughness of his skin herself. Jerking her eyes away, she forced her attention back to the conversation.

'It's…it's not going to be easy for you,' she said, and couldn't help reflecting that it obviously wasn't going to be easy for *her* either if she carried on thinking about him like that. For such an ordinary-looking man, he had an irritating ability to make her notice little details about him, like the texture of his skin, or the shape of his brows, or that intriguing shadow where his jaw met his neck beneath his ear…

'I wish Kathryn could have been there.' Nat, oblivious to her scrutiny, was following his own train of thought. 'I'm worried about the Ashcrofts,' he confided. 'They're from the generation that thinks men are incapable of looking after children. I promised that I would take Kathryn to meet them, and even though I can make some excuse to explain why she's not with me I think they're going to be disappointed.'

His mouth pulled down at the corners as he imagined the Ashcrofts' reaction. 'It's going to be difficult enough for them as it is, without them fretting about who exactly is going to be looking after William and Daisy.'

Nat had all of Prue's attention now. Very carefully, she put her mug down on the table. She had decided that her idea wasn't worth mentioning but, if Nat himself had raised the problem, surely it was worth a try? He could only say no.

'Would it make a big difference if you did have your fiancée with you?'

'Not to me,' he said, 'but to the Ashcrofts. I think it would have made it a lot easier for them to hand Laura's children into the care of a couple. They would have been able to imagine Kathryn being a mother to their grand-children but—' Nat broke off and shrugged. 'Well, it can't be helped,' he finished abruptly.

'What if it *could* be helped?' said Prue, and he looked at her in surprise.

'What do you mean?'

'I mean, perhaps you should make sure the Ashcrofts *do* meet your fiancée.'

Nat's face closed. 'I can't ask Kathryn to come with me,' he said flatly.

'I wasn't thinking of her,' said Prue. She took a deep breath. It was now or never. 'I was thinking of me.'

At least she had the satisfaction of startling Nat. She had been wondering what it would take to shake him, and now she knew.

'*What?*'

She moistened her lips. 'I could be your fiancée,' she said, quaking inwardly but determined not to show it. 'Just pretend, of course,' she added hastily as Nat opened his mouth. 'The Ashcrofts wouldn't recognise Kathryn, would they?'

'No.' Nat was watching her in wary amazement, but there seemed no reason not to answer her question. 'They were in no state to take in anything I said after the funeral. I doubt if they would even remember her name.'

'Well, then,' said Prue. 'If we told them that we were engaged, they would believe us. You could introduce me as your fiancée instead of a temporary nanny, and they would be much happier about handing over William and Daisy to the two of us, wouldn't they?'

'But I couldn't ask you to take on a pretence like that, Prue,' Nat objected. 'You'll be doing enough by helping me with William and Daisy on the plane.'

Prue got to her feet and went to stand by the verandah rail, with her back to him. She ran a finger along the worn wood. 'The thing is,' she confessed at last, 'it would quite suit me to have a fiancé myself in London.'

There was a long pause. Prue closed her eyes, hearing her words still ringing in the silence and wishing desperately that she could call them back.

It was too late for that now, though. She stayed very still, unable to turn round and meet Nat's eyes, and in the end he came to join her at the rail. To her relief, he didn't exclaim or laugh or stare. He just leant on the rail and looked out at the palm fronds.

'I think you'd better explain,' he said.

'It's my own fault,' said Prue in a low voice. 'I've been stupid, and I've got myself into a mess, and I thought you might be able to get me out of it—but I wouldn't blame you if you didn't want to!'

'Why don't you tell me what it is, and then I'll see what I can do?' suggested Nat calmly, and she turned round so that she was leaning back against the rail and didn't have to watch his face while she told her pathetic story.

'I've always been the odd one out in my family,' she began with apparent irrelevance. 'Cleo and Marisa— that's my older sister—are very alike. They're both very pretty, very clever, very popular. They're good at everything they do.' Prue smiled wryly. 'And the worst thing is, they're both wonderful. I love them dearly, but sometimes it's hard being the ugly duckling of the family.'

Nat turned his head so that he could study her profile. She had a fine bone structure, and although he could see that her features weren't classically perfect they were put together with a quirkiness that had a charm all of its own and that would last much longer than superficial beauty.

'No one could call you ugly,' he said almost roughly, and she flushed.

'Thank you,' she said, but avoided his eyes. 'I didn't really mean that I was ugly in terms of looks, though. It's more the way I never seem to fit into the family. It's not that they don't love me—I know they do—but they think I'm a bit odd. Cleo and Marisa are strictly city girls. Neither of them would know what to do with themselves in the outback. Maybe that's one of the reasons I love it here so much,' she went on slowly, as the thought oc-

curred to her for the first time. 'I know that this is one
place where neither of my sisters would come and out-
shine me.'

'They couldn't do that.'

'They could,' said Prue. 'It wouldn't be deliberate, but
they're so beautiful and such fun, and they've got a sort
of aura about them. They *dazzle*…I don't really know
how to explain it,' she admitted helplessly, 'but if Cleo,
say, was here now, you wouldn't notice me at all.'

Nat let his gaze rest on Prue's averted face, on the
dark, downcast lashes and the fine skin and the curve of
her mouth. He found it very hard to believe that he would
ever not notice her.

'I suppose I hoped that by going away I'd be the ugly
duckling who turned into a swan,' she was saying with
a rueful smile. 'I wanted to find a place where I belonged,
and I wasn't just poor old Prue with her funny ideas
about living in the back of beyond. And then one day I
had a letter from Cleo telling me all about the wedding
and how everything was perfect for her and I…well, I
wanted her to know that things could be perfect for me,
too.'

Prue risked a glance at Nat to see how he was taking
this stumbling story, but it was hard to read anything in
those deep brown eyes. At least he was listening, though.

Surreptitiously moistening her lips, she made herself
go on. 'I was so in love with Ross, and the first time he
kissed me it was like a dream come true. I had to tell
someone how wonderful he was, so I wrote back to Cleo
and said that I'd met this fantastic man, and how happy
I was.'

She flushed, remembering how she had poured her
heart out to Cleo. 'I suppose I got a bit carried away,'
she told Nat, shame-faced. 'I was so sure that things

would work out with Ross that I hinted that I'd be getting married myself and that I might not come to the wedding alone. It was just fantasy, I know, but there didn't seem any harm in it. I knew what the wedding would be like— full of cousins commiserating that my younger sister was getting married before me, and aunts assuring me that it would be ''your turn next, dear'', and all Cleo's friends wondering why I was wasting my life in the outback.' Prue pulled a face at the thought.

'And then...' She turned round and laid her hands on the rail, wondering if Nat would have any conception of what had driven her to do what she had done. 'Then I let myself imagine what it would be like if I could walk into that wedding with Ross. He would have been a sensation,' she said a little sadly, remembering how vividly she had pictured the scene.

Ross at her side, so handsome, so sexy, so different from the pallid city men. If he'd walked into the wedding he would have brought a whiff of wide horizons with him, an air of being ready to throw himself onto a horse at the slightest provocation and gallop off in a cloud of dust. No one would have thought of her as 'poor old Prue' if Ross had been with her.

Prue sighed. 'It was pathetic, I know, but there didn't seem to be any harm in dreaming. The only trouble was that I'd posted my letter to Cleo before I began to realise that Ross wasn't thinking along the same lines at all. The next thing I knew Cleo had written back, agog for more details. If I'd had any sense, I would have told her then that it didn't look as if it was going to work out after all, but I just couldn't.' Prue looked at Nat, the silver eyes pleading for his understanding. 'I couldn't admit to Cleo that the love of my life had only lasted two weeks. It was much easier to let her carry on thinking that I was blissfully happy, and tell her in a few months time that it hadn't worked out after all.'

'So Cleo and the rest of your family are still expecting you to turn up at the wedding with Ross?' said Nat carefully, not sure that he was following the precise line of Prue's reasoning.

'Yes.' Prue had suddenly run out of steam, and her shoulders slumped.

Nat was beginning to see where this was leading. 'And you can't ask Ross to go with you?'

'How can I?' she demanded. 'I can't think of a situation more guaranteed to make a man run a mile in the opposite direction than to ask him to pretend to be in love with you because you've told everyone that he already is!'

'You're asking me.' It wasn't even a question.

There was a short silence, and then Prue nodded.

'It would be different with you,' she tried to explain.

'Why?'

'Because I'm not in love with you.'

He had asked for that, Nat thought wryly.

'And you're not in love with me,' Prue hurried on. 'I was going to tell Cleo that Ross was too busy on the station to come and hope that she believed me, but when you offered me the job as nanny, and I thought about the fact that we were going to be in London at the same time, it seemed *meant*, somehow.

'I'm desperate,' she admitted, when Nat didn't say anything. 'I've got to go to the wedding, but now they're all expecting me to roll up with a gorgeous Australian bloke, and I just wondered…'

'If I would be Ross?'

CHAPTER FOUR

'WOULD you mind?' said Prue, hoping that she didn't sound too desperate. 'It would just be for the wedding.'

What was she thinking? Of *course* she sounded desperate. How did she get herself into these situations? Prue wondered in despair. Nat must think that she was absolutely pathetic, writing to her sister about a fantasy love affair, as if she were a silly schoolgirl instead of a grown woman.

And he'd be right. She *was* pathetic.

Nat's silence was unnerving. He was obviously trying to find a kind way of refusing her. Or maybe even of telling her that he didn't want her as a nanny any more! Rapidly losing her nerve, Prue gripped the verandah rail and wondered how she could ever have expected him to agree.

'Look, don't worry,' she blurted out at last, unable to bear the suspense any longer. 'It was a really stupid idea. Forget it.' Pinning a bright smile on her face, she stepped back from the rail. 'Can I go and have a look at the river?'

'Hold on,' said Nat calmly, and put out a hand to stop her as she turned. His fingers closed around her wrist, and her heart lurched alarmingly at his touch. 'I haven't said that I won't do it.'

He let go of her almost immediately, and Prue was surprised to see when she looked down that his fingers had left no mark on her skin. 'There's no reason why you should get involved in my silly little problems,' she

said uncertainly, holding her wrist as if he had hurt her.
'You've got more important things to think about.'

'One of them is how the Ashcrofts are going to react
when I take William and Daisy away,' Nat pointed out.
'I've been thinking about what you said. You were right.
If you were to pretend to be my fiancée it would make
it a lot easier for everyone, and I reckon pretending to
be your fiancé in return is the least I could do. I'm not
sure you've really thought it through, though.'

Prue was too relieved that he hadn't dismissed the idea
out of hand to object to his implied criticism. Of course
it wouldn't be the same as walking in with Ross, but with
Nat at her side she would at least be spared the humiliation of having to explain to Cleo that her wonderful love
affair had come to nothing.

'What do you mean?' she asked.

'I don't think I'd make a very convincing Ross, for a
start.'

'You wouldn't have to be him,' she reassured him eagerly. 'I didn't trust Cleo not to ring Cowen Creek in the
middle of the night and demand to interrogate him, so I
never gave her a name. All she knows is that he's an
Australian and that his family owns a cattle station. You
could just be yourself.'

'You must have described him, didn't you?'

'I said he was incredibly attractive,' Prue admitted, trying to remember exactly what she had told Cleo. Had she
talked about Ross's fair hair and blue eyes or just raved
generally about how gorgeous he was?

'Oh, I see what you mean,' she said as the penny finally dropped. 'You mean that Cleo might be surprised
when you turn up? I don't think it'll matter too much,
though,' she added without thinking. 'You're Australian,
that's the main thing. That should be enough.'

Too late, Prue heard what she had said, and her hand flew to her mouth. It hadn't been very complimentary, implying as it had that Nat had only his nationality to recommend him.

'I didn't mean...' she stammered in consternation. 'I mean, it's not that you're *not*...'

She looked so embarrassed that Nat's mouth twitched. 'It's all right,' he said. 'I know what you mean!'

He kept his face straight, but Prue was relieved to see the smile glinting in his brown eyes. 'If you think my accent will be enough to convince your sisters, I'm quite happy to pretend to be engaged to you in London.'

'*Really*?'

'I can't hide William and Daisy, though,' he pointed out. 'How will your family react to them?'

Prue wrinkled her nose. She hadn't thought about the twins. 'I'll explain the situation when I ask if anyone knows of a house you could rent for a month. They'll be a good reason for us not to stay with my parents, now I come to think of it. With any luck, they'll be so taken up with Cleo's wedding that they won't have too much time to think about us anyway and, if they do arrange anything, you can always use the twins as an excuse to slope off.'

It sounded fair enough to Nat. 'Well, if we're agreed, I'll book the flight and a hotel for the first couple of nights next week.'

'I'm...terribly grateful,' said Prue, hardly able to believe that it was all going to work out just as she had wanted. 'I can't tell you what it's going to mean to me.'

Nat looked down into her eager face. The grey eyes were shining, and he felt his throat tighten. 'It's going to mean a lot to me, too,' he said quietly.

But not the same as it did to her, obviously. To Prue,

their mock engagement meant only saving face with her family, the last cloud vanishing off the horizon so that she could look forward to coming back to Ross with un-interrupted pleasure, while to him it would mean long days in her warm, quirky presence, growing used to the way she pushed her hair behind her ears, learning what made her smile…

No, that wasn't right! Nat slammed the brakes on his drifting thoughts, and frowned. Anyone would think he was going to do something stupid like fall in love with her, which he wasn't.

Absolutely, definitely not.

He had more important things to think about, as Prue herself had pointed out. No, he was simply grateful to her for helping him out with William and Daisy, and for making it easier for him to reassure the Ashcrofts that he would be able to care for their grandchildren. That was all their so-called engagement meant to him.

Prue saw his brows draw together, and the strange ex-pression in his eyes made her wonder if Nat was already having doubts.

'I hope that pretending to be engaged isn't going to put you in an awkward situation,' she said guiltily, be-latedly realising that she had been so wrapped up in her own situation that she hadn't given much thought to what effect it might have on Nat.

'In what way?'

'Well…the Grangers told me about you and Kathryn,' said Prue hesitantly. 'It would be awful if she heard that we were supposedly engaged, and misunderstood.'

Nat looked down into her sympathetic eyes. She was really very sweet, he found himself thinking. There was something touching in her romantic belief in the power of love, and he didn't want to be the one to disillusion her.

It would be much easier for Prue to think that he was still in love with Kathryn, Nat decided. They were going to be spending a lot of time together, and she wouldn't be comfortable if she thought there was any chance of him taking advantage of their enforced intimacy. She had made it clear that she was only interested in Ross, and he would let her believe that he was still hoping for a reconciliation with Kathryn. At least that way they could be friends.

'You don't need to worry about Kathryn,' he said, tearing his eyes from Prue's face and turning to lean on the rail once more, his hands clasped loosely in front of him. 'She knows how I feel about her.'

'The Grangers are all sure that she really loves you, too,' said Prue. 'Mrs Granger said that the two of you belong together.' A wistful note crept into her voice. Somehow it was hard to imagine anyone ever saying that she and Ross belonged together in the same way. 'It must be wonderful to be in love and know that you're meant to be together.'

Nat watched a flock of cockatoos wheel in the air before settling back into the trees down by the river, and he thought about Kathryn. Kathryn with her witchy green eyes and her dazzling smile. Wilful, unpredictable, irresistible Kathryn. Kathryn who had walked away when he'd needed her most.

It still surprised him how easily he had accepted her decision. He had been so used to thinking of himself as in love with her that it had come as something of a shock to realise that he was quite happy after all to just be friends, and there had even been a slight, guilty sense of relief. Kathryn was what was known as a high-

maintenance female. She demanded a lot of attention. Nat
didn't think that he could have managed to run a cattle
station, look after two small babies *and* indulge her
whims.

'Wonderful,' he agreed.

Prue didn't hear the dryness in his voice. 'Ross says
she's very beautiful,' she said.

'Kathryn? Yes, she is.' There was no doubt about that,
thought Nat. 'She's the most beautiful woman I've ever
met.'

His voice was quite dispassionate and Prue glanced at
him curiously. Clearly he wasn't the type to wax lyrical
about the love of his life, but still, she would have expected him to have sounded a bit more enthusiastic when
he talked about Kathryn. Even Ross had been more el-
oquent. Depressingly so, in fact.

But Nat was a very private man, she remembered, and
a proud one. Kathryn must have hurt him very badly and,
although she was only offering sympathy, he might not
like the idea that she was picking over his hurts. Perhaps
he was trying to discourage her from asking any more.

'Oh, well...I hope it works out for you both,' she said
a little awkwardly. 'I'd hate it if my idea ended up spoil-
ing everything.'

'It won't do that.' To Prue's relief, he smiled. Not the
smile that made her heart behave so alarmingly, but still
a smile. 'But maybe it would be best not to tell Kathryn
or Ross or anyone else that you're going as anything
other than a nanny. Our "engagement", if we can call it
that, is only going to last a month, and it won't have
anything to do with anyone here. I think it should just be
between the two of us.'

'Deal,' said Prue gratefully, and held out her hand with

a smile that caught the breath in Nat's throat as he straightened from the rail.

'Deal,' he agreed, and was alarmed to hear that his voice was tinder-dry.

They shook hands, and then Prue, on an impulse, reached up to kiss him on the cheek. 'Thank you,' she said.

Nat could smell her hair, feel the softness of her face, the warmth of her lips grazing his skin, and he fought an overwhelming urge to pull her closer as his fingers tightened instinctively around hers.

Fortunately, Prue was already drawing away, but she was looking up at him smiling, and Nat found himself trapped in that clear grey gaze. He stood staring down at her, until her smile faded and he became aware too late that he was still holding her hand.

He dropped it abruptly.

There was an awkward silence, broken eventually by Nat, who cleared his throat. 'You said you wanted to see the river,' he said. 'I'll find you a quiet horse.'

Prue flicked the water from her hands and regarded her reflection in the cloakroom mirror at Heathrow with a jaundiced eye. She had been sitting in a plane for twenty-four hours, and it showed! Her eyes felt gritty, and the lighting in the Ladies gave her skin an unpleasant shade of orange. It was going to take more than washing her face and brushing her teeth—twice!—to make her feel human again.

She thought about Nat, waiting outside in the baggage claim hall, with something close to resentment. How did he manage to look as cool and uncrushed now as he had when they'd boarded the plane to Darwin at Mathison airport?

It might be something to do with his extraordinary ability to sit relaxed and patient for long stretches of time. Prue had never flown business class before and, remembering her flight out to Australia without affection, she had been thrilled with the extra space at first. But as the hours had passed she had been less and less able to get comfortable.

Fidgeting next to Nat, Prue had been very aware of how close he was. Only an arm rest away. She had shifted around in her seat, played with her headphones, tried to read and all the time her eyes had kept slipping sideways to where he sat, quiet and self-contained beside her. There had been a stillness about him that had almost been mesmerising. She had waited for him to scratch himself, or sigh with boredom, but the nearest he'd come to restlessness had been to flex his shoulders once before resettling back into his seat.

He had been wearing a short-sleeved shirt, and his bare forearm had lain on the arm rest between them. Prue had been exasperated by the way her gaze had seemed to be riveted to it, as if there was something special about the fine, dark hairs against his brown skin or the weathered leather strap of his watch. He had a broad, strong wrist, and she'd been able to see the tendons in the back of his capable hand, the faint sheen of skin over his knuckles.

It was just a hand, just an arm, she had told herself, irritated by her own fascination. Ross had an arm just like it. But it had been unsettling to realise that she had never stared at his in the same way. She had never counted the lines across the joints of his fingers and she didn't know if he had any scars like the thin, pale one running across the edge of Nat's hand. But then, she had never been trapped next to Ross for so many hours with nothing else to do, either.

Prue hadn't been able to concentrate on another thing. She had tried to sleep, but it had been impossible to relax. Nat, of course, had slept the way he did everything else: without any fuss or fidgeting or sprawling or snoring. She had watched enviously as he'd simply tipped back his seat, folded his arms and closed his eyes. In no time at all, his long body had been utterly relaxed and his breathing deep and slow.

It had been a long, boring flight, but at least it was over now. They were just waiting for their cases to appear and then they could go. Prue wished that Cleo hadn't insisted on coming to meet them. She would have preferred a long sleep so that she felt less like a zombie before she had to face her sister's inevitable interrogation.

She gave her hands a final shake and the unaccustomed glint of diamonds caught her eye. Prue grimaced as she looked down at the ring on her finger. To add the final touch to the pretence they had agreed, Nat had bought her a supposed engagement ring during their stopover at Singapore airport.

It had seemed a good idea at the time, but she couldn't get used to the feel of the ring on her third finger, and, the longer she wore it the more uncomfortable she began to feel about what they were doing. During those long, sleepless hours on the plane, Prue had had plenty of time to think about the pitfalls that lay ahead. Pretending to be engaged wasn't going to be nearly as easy as it had seemed when they had discussed it that day at Mack River.

There was nothing to get nervous about, Prue told herself, resolutely drying her hands. All she had to do was treat it as a job.

A job where they had to pretend to be in love with each other.

What could be so hard about that?

The baggage claim hall had been relatively quiet when Prue went into the Ladies but when she emerged it seemed as if at least another five long-haul flights had disgorged their passengers, and they were now milling around, jabbering and gesticulating in a babble of languages, or leaning wearily on their trolleys.

She couldn't see Nat at all. Fighting her way through the crowds to the carousel where they had been told to wait, she looked wildly around her before spotting him half hidden behind a pillar.

At the sight of his rangy figure Prue felt her momentary panic subside, and she stopped, taking a deep breath to calm herself as her eyes rested on him. He wasn't doing anything to draw attention to himself, he was just looking towards the flaps in the wall where their luggage was due to appear, but somehow he was the still, certain centre of the chaos swirling around him and, without warning, Prue's heart did a long, slow somersault, landing back in place with a thud that left her with a dizzy, oddly hollow feeling.

She stood as if rooted to the spot, staring at him as if she had never seen him before, and then the carousel jerked abruptly into life and there was a surge of expectation as the other passengers tried to manoeuvre their trolleys closer. Nat looked round and lifted a hand as he saw Prue.

'Are you OK?' he asked as she made her way to his side. 'You look a bit odd.'

'Jet lag,' she said. That was *all* it was, she told herself. 'I didn't sleep a wink on the plane.'

Nat remembered waking at one point to find Prue leaning against him, heavy with sleep. Her face had been pressed into his shoulder and a few wayward curls had tickled his jaw. He could still feel the relaxed warmth of her body, but he didn't think he would tell her that.

He turned back to the carousel, where the first cases were juddering towards them. 'It shouldn't be too much longer now,' he said instead. 'You'll be able to sleep at the hotel.'

Prue stared at a battered blue suitcase that was moving past, besplattered with stickers. 'I wish Cleo wasn't meeting us,' she blurted out.

'She wants to see you,' said Nat mildly.

'It's not me she wants to see, it's you! She can't wait to inspect you!' Prue sighed. 'I don't think you realise what's going to hit you.'

'Relax. It'll be fine.'

It was all right for Nat to tell her to relax, Prue thought edgily. He didn't know what her family was like!

She had been so taken up with getting through the ordeal of the wedding, she realised, that she hadn't really thought about what else might be involved, but now, with the prospect of coming face to face with Cleo any minute, the full realisation hit her in horrifying detail.

What had she been thinking of? Cleo's wedding wouldn't be enough to stop her mother and sisters wanting to know every detail about her engagement. They would scrutinise what Nat looked like, what he was wearing, the way he behaved, and he would face an interrogation that would put the Inquisition to shame.

And then they would sit him down and make him look at photographs of her as a baby, and tell him stories about when she was little.

Prue cringed at the very idea. Could she really put Nat through all that?

'I'm not sure pretending to be engaged is such a good idea,' she said in a hollow voice.

Nat glanced at her. She was looking tired and grumpy, but he remembered the soft warmth of her body as she had slept against him and her smile as she walked under the great gum trees at Mack River, and he felt something shift inside him.

'Do you want to change your mind?'

Did she? Prue fidgeted with the trolley. Changing her mind would mean walking out of here and telling Cleo the truth, that she had made up her engagement and that she would be going alone to the wedding. There would be no going back then.

It wasn't so much admitting that she had been stupid as what would follow, she realised. Cleo would want to know why she had roped Nat into her pretence, and there would be endless questions, and with every one she would feel smaller and sillier.

'No,' she told Nat. 'I don't, not really. It's just…do you really think we can carry it off?'

'Why not?' Nat kept half an eye on the carousel, not wanting to miss their cases when they finally appeared. 'There's no reason why your family shouldn't believe us when we say we're engaged, just like the Ashcrofts will.'

'But that's just it! Laura's parents are going to be preoccupied by other things, and I'm sure it will be enough to turn up with a ring on my finger and tell them we're getting married, but that won't be enough for Cleo and Marisa! They'll both be on the lookout for the way we behave together, and they'll want to know *everything*. If they sense something's not quite right, they'll be on to us immediately.'

'Then we'll just have to convince them that everything is all right,' said Nat.

His calm confidence irritated Prue. 'Easier said than done! It's going to take more than a ring to convince my sisters that we're in love. I don't think you realise what you're getting into,' she said honestly.

Nat had spotted one of their cases. 'You said yourself that I'm not going to spend much time with them,' he pointed out, watching its approach.

'I know, but when you do...' She trailed off, wondering quite how to put it. 'Well, you might find yourself in an embarrassing situation,' she finished awkwardly.

Lifting the case off the carousel, Nat placed it on the trolley. To Prue's chagrin, he looked faintly amused. 'What do you mean by embarrassing?'

'You know.' Prue hesitated, twisting the diamond ring around her finger. 'We're going to have to act as if we're in love. They'll be suspicious if we don't...if we don't...' She stopped and cleared her throat. 'Look, all I'm trying to say is that you might have to be prepared to...well, to...'

'To kiss you?'

The breath leaked out of Prue's lungs. 'Yes,' she managed, although it came out as more of a gasp. 'That kind of thing, anyway.'

Nat looked at her. She was rigid with embarrassment, her chin up as she stared fiercely ahead, her cheeks flushed and the wayward brown hair pushed haphazardly away from her face, and he felt something unlock inside him.

'I think I could manage that.'

The lurking smile in his voice deepened the colour in Prue's cheeks. He thought that she was being ridiculous, but she was only thinking of him forcing himself to kiss her when he was in love with Kathryn. She gritted her teeth. 'I can see it might be difficult for you, that's all,' she ploughed on.

'What's difficult about a kiss?' said Nat. 'Look, I'll

show you,' he went on, seeing that Prue was unconvinced.

He reached out an unhurried hand and laid it gently against her face, and for Prue it was as if everything had stopped. The hustle and bustle of the airport, the shuddering conveyor belt, even the blood in her veins seemed to freeze. She couldn't move, couldn't breathe, could just stand there, mouse-still, with Nat's palm cool and strong against her cheek and his thumb tracing the line of her lower lip almost thoughtfully.

'It's easy,' he said softly, curving his hand around her throat, sliding it beneath her hair to the nape of her neck, drawing her slowly, irresistibly towards him.

After that first moment of paralysis, Prue's body slammed back into overdrive. Her heart was lurching around her chest, her pulse boomed in her ears and she churned with a terrifying mixture of nerves and anticipation. When Nat bent his head, she closed her eyes against the treacherous thrill that shot through her as his mouth came down on hers. The touch of his lips was warm and sure and somehow right. Prue was conscious of a disturbing sense of recognition, as if she had always known that his kiss would feel like this, as if her lips were meant to part beneath his, as if her arms had been waiting for the chance to hold him.

Her hands lifted instinctively to clutch at his chest, but even as she leant closer Nat was lifting his head, letting his hand fall from her neck.

'I didn't find that too difficult,' he said calmly. 'Did you?'

Dazed and disorientated, Prue could only stare up at him. She felt as if she had been shown a tantalising glimpse of something deep and dark and dangerously exciting, only to have the door slammed shut again in her face, and she didn't know whether to be disappointed or relieved.

She swallowed painfully. 'N-no,' she managed to croak. It was as if the world had slipped out of kilter during those few seconds when Nat's lips had been on hers. She could see and hear still but the world around her seemed unreal, faintly blurry at the edges, and she blinked in a desperate attempt to bring it all into focus.

Nat smiled, and his gaze flickered downwards to where her fingers were still curled into his shirt. He didn't say anything but he might as well have thrown a bucket of cold water over her. Jerked back to reality, Prue snatched her hands away, blushing furiously.

'Of course not,' she added coldly to disguise how mortified she felt.

Nat was as unmoved by the chill in her voice as he had been by the kiss, Prue realised, eying him with resentment. 'There's your case,' he said casually, and reached past her to pluck it from the carousel and put it on the trolley.

He turned back to Prue. 'Ready?'

Of course she wasn't ready! she wanted to shout. She wasn't even sure that she could stand up without the trolley to hang on to, let alone walk out of here and face Cleo, with her searching questions and her sharp eyes, but she couldn't tell Nat that. If she told him that her knees were wobbling and her heart was thudding and every nerve in her body was fluttering he would think that it was because of that brief, impersonal kiss of his, which it couldn't be, of course.

It was just the effect of a long flight. Her body was confused after passing through all those time zones, that was all it was. It was absolutely nothing to do with him.

Fixing a bright smile on her face, Prue nodded. 'Let's go.'

Nat took the trolley, and they walked through Customs and suddenly were out in the hubbub of the arrivals hall. A confusion of faces greeted them as people pressed against the barrier, watching eagerly for their loved ones to appear, and tearful reunions blocked the exit.

Overwhelmed, Prue hesitated. She was still strumming from that unexpected kiss, reeling from noise and tiredness. She had an impulse to turn back and hide, but Nat kept on walking and she had to hurry to catch him up.

'What—?' he began, with a quick glance of concern, but suddenly Cleo was there, smiling, hugging her excitedly, talking nineteen to the dozen.

'Oh, Prue, it's so good to see you! How brown you look! Did you have a good flight? I made Alex get up at five so that we'd get here in good time.'

Prue was used to her sister and didn't even try to reply to the bombardment of questions. 'Hello, Cleo. Hello, Alex,' she said, kissing them both.

Cleo was blonde and beautiful, with perfect teeth and perfect skin and sparkling blue eyes. Her fiancé was the same height as Nat, but there the resemblance between the two men ended. Alex, sleek and suave and immaculately groomed, was darkly handsome with an unmistakable sheen of prosperity about him. He looked exactly what he was: an extremely successful financial analyst. Prue had always thought the two of them could pose as an illustration of the perfect couple.

They were both looking at Nat with undisguised curiosity and he nodded pleasantly in return, unfazed by their stares.

Prue turned too, trying to see him through their eyes, a lean brown man with a quiet face and watchful eyes.

Cleo and Alex would think him unremarkable, she knew. They couldn't tell that behind his apparent insignificance lay a strength and assurance they could only ever dream of. They didn't know his calm competence, or the easy way he moved through the land as if he were part of it, or the slow smile that gathered in the back of his brown eyes.

'This is Nat,' she said weakly.

Cleo moved past her to envelop Nat in a scented hug. 'It's lovely to meet you,' she told him, giving him the full benefit of her beautiful eyes. 'Prue's been so vague in her letters that we were beginning to wonder if you really existed!'

Fortunately, she didn't wait for an answer, but flitted back to Alex. 'This is Alex, my fiancé. We're both so thrilled you could come to the wedding with Prue after all.'

The two men shook hands. Watching nervously, Prue could see that Alex was unimpressed. His eyes flickered dismissively over Nat's plain shirt and moleskin trousers and checked out his watch and boots, but there was plainly not a single brand he recognised.

'Congratulations,' he said to Nat, pumping his hand a little too heartily. 'I hear you're taking the plunge, too. Happens to the best of us, eh?'

'We're all *so* excited about your engagement,' Cleo put in, beaming. 'Mum and Marisa were very jealous that I was going to meet you first. We've all been longing to know what you were like. We couldn't believe it when Prue wrote and said that she was getting married.' She grinned affectionately at her sister. 'Somehow she's never seemed the type.'

Nat followed her gaze to Prue, who stood with her chin tilted and a determined smile that didn't disguise for a minute that she was hating every moment of this. He could still feel the softness of her hair against his hand and the piercing sweetness of her lips, and he wondered if she had any idea of how much it had cost him to break the kiss then instead of yanking her roughly into his arms as he had wanted to do.

Reaching out, Nat smoothed a stray strand of hair behind her ear. He was only acting the part he had agreed, he told himself, letting his hand linger against her throat. He looked directly at Cleo, who obviously didn't believe that Prue was the type men fell in love with and married.

'She is to me,' he said.

CHAPTER FIVE

DETERMINED to find some common masculine ground with Nat, Alex led the way to the car park talking about cars and managing to spend quite a bit of time boasting about his new Porsche.

'She's a little beauty,' he told Nat. 'I'd have brought her this morning, but Cleo insisted on the BMW instead because she thought there wouldn't be enough room for everyone. Nonsense, of course, but you know what women are like! The Porsche would have been fine, but I'll take you for a spin later,' he promised, and it was obvious he could offer no greater treat.

Following behind with Cleo, her skin still burning where Nat's fingers had grazed her face, Prue listened tensely. Alex was all right when you got past the bluff, but he was bound to try and patronise Nat.

Not that Nat showed much sign of being impressed. If the thought of being driven around in Alex's precious Porsche excited him he gave no sign of it, merely thanking him with a calmness that Alex clearly found incomprehensible.

There was a short silence. 'What do you drive?' he asked after a moment, sounding put out.

'A ute, mostly.'

Alex looked blank. He needed a label, a designer—something he could relate to. 'What's that?'

'A utility truck. It's a good vehicle for rough country.'

'Ah, yes. I forgot that you were a farmer,' said Alex

patronisingly, eyeing Nat as if wondering why he didn't have a straw sticking out of his mouth.

Prue's fingernails dug into her palm. 'Mack River is a cattle station, not a farm,' she said sharply.

'Big place?' Alex asked Nat, ignoring her.

'Not particularly,' said Nat.

'How big is that exactly?'

'About two and a half thousand.'

Prue could see Alex preparing to cap Nat's answer with tales of his grand landowning friends. 'Acres?'

Nat glanced at him. 'Square kilometres.'

Prue relaxed slightly and smiled. Nat, she thought, was more than capable of dealing with Alex.

Beside her, Cleo raised her brows in the direction of Nat's back and tucked her arm through Prue's. 'He's not very chatty, is he?' she said in an undertone.

'He's tired,' Prue bristled, instantly on the defensive. 'And anyway, he only talks when he's got something to say,' she went on defiantly. *Unlike Alex*, she would have liked to add, but didn't. She had only just arrived, after all, and it was too soon to start arguing with Cleo.

'Hmn…the strong, silent type, is he?'

'Something like that,' said Prue, knowing that it would be hopeless trying to explain Nat to someone like Cleo.

Her sister's mouth turned down in a grimace. 'I've never understood the appeal of silence,' she said frankly. 'Doesn't it get a bit boring after a while?'

Prue thought about the day she had spent at Mack River with Nat, how he had ridden patiently beside her through the scrub, pointing out birds and plants she had never seen before, how he had looked, outlined against the horizon in the crystalline light, how he had smiled beneath his hat.

And then she thought about the way he had kissed her

by the carousel, and her heart began to boom and thud at the memory. Whatever else it had been, it hadn't been boring.

'No,' she said, dry-voiced. 'Nat's never boring.'

'Oh? Well, as long as you don't think so.' Cleo was patently unconvinced. 'I must say, I'm a bit disappointed. I thought we'd be getting Crocodile Dundee!' The blue eyes surveyed Nat critically. 'I wouldn't call him much of a looker.'

Prue pulled her arm out of Cleo's and glared at her sister. 'What do you mean?' she demanded.

'There's no need to ruffle up like that!' said Cleo, amused. 'I'm sure he's very nice. I'm only saying that he's not what I expected. You made out in your letters that he was absolutely gorgeous!'

Prue bit her lip. She had forgotten for a moment that she had been talking about Ross when she wrote those letters. Cleo wouldn't have been disappointed in Ross if he'd been there with her.

But Ross wasn't there, and Nat was, and she would have to be careful that Cleo didn't get suspicious. 'Nat may not be obvious,' she said slowly, 'but when you get to know him, he's...'

She trailed off, picturing him as he had been that afternoon at Mack River: his stillness, the strength in his hands, the ease with which he'd swung himself onto his horse.

'I think he's very attractive,' she finished lamely.

Cleo laughed as she took Prue's arm affectionately once more. 'You must be in love!' she said.

Automatically, Prue opened her mouth to deny any such thing, and only just managed to stop herself in time. She was *supposed* to sound as if she were in love with

Nat, she reminded herself. If they were going to go through with this pretence, she might as well do it properly.

'I am,' she said as coolly as she could, and was then afraid that she had sounded too cool, for Cleo was looking at her with a very strange expression. 'Tell me about the wedding,' she said, hastily changing the subject. 'Are you all organised?'

Cleo needed no encouragement and chattered happily about the arrangements all the way out of Heathrow and along the M4. Bridesmaids...flowers...music... photographs... The words flowed over Prue's head, and all she had to do was put in the occasional 'Oh, really?' to make it sound as if she were listening.

It was nearly half past seven, and the early-morning traffic was already clogging up the roads. Caught in the frustrating business of stopping and starting, darting through a sudden clear patch and then grinding to a halt once more, Prue thought longingly of the empty outback roads, where you raised a hand in greeting to every vehicle that passed.

Once, not so long ago, all this had been familiar to Prue, but now it felt alien, like visiting another planet. The colours were different in London. Here, everything was grey, with sudden splashes of startling green, and even though the sky was clear it was a pale, soft, washed-out kind of blue, nothing like the fierce Australian sky.

It was all different, thought Prue. The cars around them were smaller and less rugged than the ones she was used to seeing, and their yellow licence plates looked strange. Even the road signs, marking the turn-offs to places Prue had once known well, seemed—

She sat up abruptly. 'This isn't the way to the hotel!'

she said, breaking into Cleo's reasons for choosing a finger buffet over a sit-down meal.

'We're not going to the hotel,' Cleo told her. 'I cancelled your reservation.'

'You did *what*?'

'You didn't really think we would let you come to London and stay in a *hotel*, did you? No, I arranged it all with Mum ages ago. You're staying with us.'

'But, Cleo—'

'It's all organised,' said Cleo, waving Prue's protests down. 'Marisa and Phil and the kids can stay with Mum and Dad, and you're staying with us. We've got a spare room, and it'll give us a chance to see you before you disappear back off to Australia. Besides,' she went on gaily, 'I had this brilliant idea!'

Prue's heart sank. How were they going to get out of this? 'Oh?'

'You know you asked me about house-sitting? Well, the answer's obvious! You can use my flat. We're going to be on honeymoon for two and a half weeks, so you can have it to yourselves. You can drive my car, too, if you want. It'll mean we don't need to worry about security, and you won't need to worry about getting used to a stranger's house.'

'The thing is, we're going to have William and Daisy with us,' Prue tried with a hint of desperation. 'They're the babies I told you about, and you know how much mess babies make.'

'Oh, that's no problem,' said Cleo. 'We're going to sell the flat when we get back anyway. Alex has already sold his, and if we get a good price for mine we can buy a decent house with a garden. So don't worry if the kids are sick on the carpets or anything. It might be better if they don't come and stay until after the wedding, of course, but only because we've got a busy week coming up.'

Swivelling round from the front seat, Cleo looked curiously at her sister. 'I thought you'd be pleased,' she said. 'You know what Mum's like about separate bedrooms! She does try not to be old-fashioned, but the one time Alex and I stayed there together she made such an effort to be good about it that it was excruciating. Honestly, I'd rather Alex had slept on the sofa! Believe me,' she assured Prue, 'you'll be much better off with us.'

'I'm sorry about this,' Prue said to Nat when Cleo had shown them into the spare room with a flourish and left them to put on some coffee. They could hear her in the kitchen just along the corridor, sending Alex out to the delicatessen on the corner to buy fresh croissants.

Prue stood awkwardly by the door and looked at anything except the bed. It dominated the room, a double certainly, but not a big one, and the thought of sleeping in it next to Nat was for some reason deeply uncomfortable.

'I couldn't think of any way to get out of it,' she apologised.

'There was nothing you could do,' said Nat understandingly. 'In any case, once Cleo had cancelled the hotel, we had to have somewhere to go!'

'I should have known she would do something like that,' Prue sighed with exasperation. 'I could kill her sometimes!'

'She's only trying to make you welcome.' Nat noted the fresh flowers on the chest of drawers and the bed that had been carefully made and scattered with cushions. 'She's fond of you. You can't blame her for wanting to see more of you.'

'I know, it's just frustrating the way she makes it impossible for you not to do exactly what *she* wants the whole time!'

'She reminds me of Kathryn,' said Nat, moving one of the suitcases out of the way.

Prue went very still. 'Oh?'

'Cleo doesn't look like Kathryn, of course, but she's got the same way of getting exactly what she wants.' He smiled wryly. 'You can try and refuse the Kathryns and Cleos of this world, but they're so beautiful and charming they make you feel churlish and before you know where you are you've given in, just like they knew you would all along.'

'Yes, that's Cleo. Marisa's like that, too.'

Prue was glad that Nat had reminded her about Kathryn. It helped put that brief kiss by the carousel into perspective. She had spent too much of her life in her sisters' shadow to have any illusions about her own appeal compared to the irresistible gaiety and charm of a girl like Kathryn. One little kiss was hardly going to make Nat forget his real love, was it?

Which was good, of course.

Uneasily conscious of a sinking feeling at the thought, Prue caught herself up sternly. She was very glad that she and Nat had been quite open about how they felt. Otherwise there could have been all sorts of misunderstandings when it came to things like kissing or sharing a bed.

As it was, she knew that it would take more than a quick peck to change the way Nat felt about Kathryn. Sharing a bed wasn't going to bother *him*.

If only she could believe that it wasn't going to bother her either.

The cases seemed to take up most of the room.

Stepping round them gingerly, Prue went over to the window and pretended to be interested in the garden that belonged to the flat below.

Behind her, Nat stretched out on the bed with his arms above his head and yawned. He was tired too, Prue realised and felt a bit better. This buzzing, jittery feeling was just exhaustion. She was too weary to think clearly, and as a result she had blown that stupid kiss out of proportion. Tomorrow, when she had caught up on her sleep, she would be amazed that she could have got herself in such a state about it.

The thought gave her the courage to perch on the edge of the bed, with her back to Nat. 'I shouldn't have suggested this engagement business,' she apologised, twisting the ring around her finger. 'Now look at the mess I've got us into!'

'It'll be fine,' said Nat calmly. 'This is a nice apartment, and we can bring William and Daisy here. That's all that matters to me.'

'You don't think it'll be awkward?' In spite of herself, Prue coloured painfully. 'Sharing a bed, I mean?'

Her hair swung forward, hiding her face, and her shoulders were set at a rigid angle. Nat thought about sliding across the bed and rubbing her back until she relaxed, until she could lie down beside him and let the tension evaporate. Then he thought that he had better stay right where he was. She was uncomfortable enough as it was, and he couldn't blame her. The only place she wanted to be was next to Ross, and he had better not forget it.

'It's only for a week,' he said, keeping his voice deliberately cool and impersonal. 'Like Cleo says, we'll have the place to ourselves after the wedding and we can have a bedroom each then.'

Only a week. Only a week of lying next to her, knowing she was only a few inches away. Only a week of keeping his hands firmly to himself. Nat sighed inwardly. He had a feeling that it was going to be a long week.

'I'd offer to sleep on the floor,' he went on, 'but there's not a lot of room and Cleo might think it was a bit odd if she came in.'

'There's no need for that,' Prue protested, mortified at the idea that he had picked up on how nervous she felt at the prospect of sleeping with him. She put up her chin. 'I don't mind sharing. I mean, it's not as if you're...or that we're likely to....' Floundering, she made an effort to pull herself together. 'That is, I know how you feel about Kathryn,' she tried again, a little more coherently this time.

This was clearly not the time to tell her that what he had once felt for Kathryn had gone, thought Nat ruefully. Or that what really worried him was the way he was beginning to feel about *her*.

'You don't need to worry, Prue,' he told her instead. 'I haven't forgotten the deal we made. It's not that big a bed, but there's room for both of us, and I won't...' Nat paused, searching for the right word '...take advantage,' he finished, opting for the more delicate option.

Of course he wouldn't, Prue realised. Why would he want to take advantage of her, when he was used to Kathryn with her long legs and her green eyes and her no doubt perfect skin?

She summoned a smile. 'No, I know you won't,' she said. 'I was just being silly.'

'You're just tired, that's all. You'll feel better when you've had some sleep. It's all going fine so far, isn't it?' Nat added in an attempt to cheer her up.

Prue looked at him doubtfully. 'Is it?'

'Of course it is. We've got a great flat to stay in and an ideal place to bring the twins. Cleo and Alex don't seem to have had any problem believing we're engaged, and if they don't suspect, why should anyone else? All you've got to do now is get through the wedding, and you'll have Ross to go home to.'

Nat's mouth twisted as he remembered the scene at Mathison airport, the unthinking lift of his heart when he had seen Prue walking towards him, followed by the sinking realisation that Ross was at her side. He had had to stand by and watch as the younger man gathered her into his arms for a farewell kiss.

'He seemed pretty sorry to see you go,' he reminded her. 'Or are you going to tell me that Ross kisses all their cooks goodbye like that?'

At least he had the satisfaction of seeing Prue brighten.

'He *did* say he hoped I would be able to go back to Cowen Creek, didn't he?' she remembered. 'And he asked for my number in London so that he could get in touch if he needed.'

'I bet Ross is going to miss you more than he realises,' Nat forced himself to encourage her. Hell, *he* had missed her when she had gone off on her own to buy some duty free for Cleo at Singapore, and she'd only been gone half an hour.

'Coming to London will turn out to be the best thing you could have done, you'll see,' he said.

Cleo laid on a special welcome breakfast with Bucks Fizz, freshly ground coffee and warm buttery croissants, and proceeded to lay out an exhausting week of activities she had planned for them. Prue wasn't too surprised to discover that, in spite of the fact that she had written to explain the situation with William and Daisy, Cleo was still reluctant to accept that they really had to spend so much time with the twins, but Nat handled her with an ease that was no doubt born of years of practice with Kathryn.

'Oh, all right,' Cleo grumbled, backing down at last, 'but you've got to let Prue come shopping with me one day at least! I've already arranged for her to have a fitting for her dress on Wednesday, and then she'll need some shoes. We might as well get you some decent clothes while we're out as well,' she went on, regarding her sister with a mixture of exasperation and affection. 'Haven't you got *anything* other than jeans in your wardrobe, Prue?'

'Not really,' mumbled Prue.

Nat looked at her. She was wearing a long-sleeved T-shirt with a scoop neck that showed the shadowy hollow at the base of her throat and, although her hair was tousled and her eyes looked huge with tiredness, he thought she had never looked more desirable.

'She looks fine to me,' he said.

'I'm sure she does,' said Cleo tartly, 'but she's in London now! She's going to have to have something suitable to wear in the evenings. It's not just the wedding, you know. We're having a family dinner with Mum and Dad when Marisa arrives to celebrate your engagement, and then there's Sabrina's pre-wedding party, and you can't wear your jeans to that!'

'All right, I'll come shopping with you on Wednesday,' Prue agreed, to shut her sister up. 'But the rest of the time we really do need to be with William and Daisy, Cleo.'

'I hope they'll be able to spare you on Saturday!' said Cleo huffily. 'I know it's only my wedding and that I'm only your sister, but I do think you might want to spend some time with *me*!'

It took Prue some time to charm her out of her threatened sulk, and she had to promise to go to every party the insatiably sociable Cleo had arranged that week, although her heart sank at the thought. 'Everyone wants to see you,' Cleo insisted, although Prue found it hard to believe that anyone would notice if she was there or not when her sister was in the room.

When breakfast was over, Alex got to his feet and announced that some people had work to do on a Monday morning. Prue was hoping that Cleo would be going to work too, but it seemed that her sister had taken the whole week off prior to the wedding. 'I haven't got time to work!' she said, tripping back into the kitchen after bidding her fiancé a fond farewell at the door.

'Now, Mum and Dad are coming to supper tonight, so we've got the whole day to ourselves. I need to pick up my shoes, then I've got a few jobs in town, so why don't you come with me? We could have lunch and—'

'Prue's tired,' Nat interrupted her. He had been watching her swaying in her seat, her eyes glassy with exhaustion. 'She didn't sleep on the plane.'

Cleo pursed her mouth. 'It's much better for her to stay awake, you know,' she said. 'She should keep busy and go to bed at the right time.'

'I think she would be better here with me.' There was a note of finality in Nat's voice that even Cleo recognised.

'Oh very well!' she grumbled. 'But don't blame me when she can't sleep tonight!'

Nat gave Prue nearly four hours before he judged that she had had enough. Not wanting to startle her, he sat cautiously on the edge of the bed, but she was sound asleep, her face turned into the pillow and half hidden by a tumble of brown curls.

It was a shame that she felt so overshadowed by Cleo, he thought, letting his eyes linger on the dark sweep of lashes against her cheek, the smooth, bare shoulders and the gentle rise and fall of her breathing. Prue might not have her sister's golden beauty, but he for one preferred luminous grey eyes to dazzling blue. He liked the fact that her features weren't quite symmetrical and that her hair was always untidy. He liked her elfin, expressive face and the way she always looked warm and tousled, as if she had just fallen out of bed. He liked a lot of things about her.

He just wished he could find something he didn't like. Apart from the fact that she was head over heels in love with Ross Granger, of course.

'Prue?' He ran a gentle finger down the bare arm that lay over the duvet. 'Prue, it's time to wake up.'

Prue surfaced groggily, mumbling in protest as she was dragged up through layers of deep sleep. When she finally managed to ungum her eyelids, the first thing she saw was Nat, sitting on the bed and watching her with an unreadable expression. Still swirling in sleep, it seemed too much effort to work out what he was doing there, but she knew that she was glad to see him and she smiled dreamily up at him.

Nat drew a sharp breath. 'It's half past one,' he said with an effort. 'If you sleep any longer Cleo will be right and you won't be able to sleep tonight.'

Blinking herself awake, Prue struggled up against the pillows and ran her hands through her hair. She felt worse now than she had done earlier, when she had fallen into bed in her underwear, too tired to open her case and find anything else to put on. 'Do I look as bad as I feel?' she groaned.

Nat had been trying not to think about how she looked. She had taken the duvet with her and was lying back against the pillows, her hair tumbling about her face and her honey-coloured shoulders bare except for her bra straps. He was very aware of the smooth warmth of her skin, of the huge, sleepy grey eyes and the tempting line of her clavicle, and he got abruptly to his feet.

'You'll feel fine after a shower,' he said, his voice curt.

He was right. Prue did feel a lot better once she had washed and changed into clean trousers and a fresh shirt. Almost normal, in fact.

Still combing out her hair she went to find Nat, who was in the kitchen staring in some bafflement at Cleo's gleaming chrome coffee machine.

'I was going to make you some coffee,' he said, 'but I give up! What's wrong with a jar of instant?'

Prue laughed. 'Don't let Cleo hear you say anything like that! She wouldn't allow instant coffee in the house. Here, let me,' she went on, moving him aside, and Nat watched as the machine sprang miraculously to life at her touch.

'How did you do that?' he demanded.

'Oh, we city girls have our uses,' she teased him. 'But don't worry, we'll buy a jar of instant later and smuggle it in. If we keep it in our room, and only use it when she's out, Cleo will never know!'

They laughed together until they made the mistake of looking at each other. Their eyes met and held, and for some reason their smiles faltered. With an effort, Prue looked away and concentrated on the coffee maker.

'Did you sleep at all?'

She sounded stilted, polite, the perfect hostess. Not at

all like someone who only moments ago had been laughing with him like an old friend, or who could talk casually about 'our room' as if they had been sleeping together for years.

To her relief, Nat moved away and sat down at the breakfast bar. 'I had a nap on the sofa,' he told her. 'Then I had a shower and rang the Ashcrofts to let them know that we'd arrived. I said we'd go along this afternoon to see them and the twins, but if you want to stay here and rest I'm sure they'd understand.'

Prue took a deep breath and shook her head. 'No, I want to go,' she said. She had to stop feeling self-conscious with Nat and start remembering just why she was there. Turning, she handed him a mug of coffee. 'That's what I'm here for.'

She met his gaze clearly to make sure that there would be no misunderstandings. 'I haven't forgotten that you've paid for my ticket, Nat. I'm here as a nanny, and everything else is incidental.'

Nat looked back at her, his brown eyes quite unreadable. 'I haven't forgotten either,' he said.

Having checked the Ashcrofts' address in the *A-Z*, Prue decided that it would be easiest to get the tube to Wimbledon. 'It shouldn't be too bad at this time of day,' she told Nat, who shrugged.

'You know your way around London,' he said. 'I'll follow you.'

Prue was very conscious of the grimness of the station, of the noise and the crowds and the stuffy air in the carriage. It was depressing to realise that this was her world as far as Nat and Ross were concerned. She could love the outback as much as they did, but, to them, she would always be a London girl, someone who belonged

in the big city the way they belonged under the big outback sky.

Australia seemed a million miles away as she sat on
the swaying train, reading the advertisements and avoiding eye contact like everyone else. Nat sat silently beside
her. He had left his hat behind, and was wearing mole-
skins and a pale, short-sleeved shirt, but even in this in-
nocuous outfit he managed to look out of place.

There was a toughness about him, Prue realised, a
quiet assurance that was as unmistakable as it was hard
to define. He couldn't help looking exactly what he was:
a man used to riding out to distant horizons. He didn't
belong in this cramped metal tube hurtling under the
streets of London.

Maybe Nat had thought she looked as out of place
riding through the scrub at Mack River, thought Prue
despondently.

They had to change trains at Earl's Court. Nat followed
obediently when she jumped out, and stood beside her
on the platform, although clearly puzzled as to why they
had got off one train only to stand and wait for another
in exactly the same place. When the next train rattled in
he glanced at Prue, but she shook her head, just as she
did for the next two.

'This one,' she said as the fourth one arrived.

Nat grimaced. 'I'm glad you're with me,' he acknowledged. 'You don't seem to need to look at anything. How
do you know where you're going?'

'The same way you know the best place to cross the
creeks at Mack River,' said Prue, who had simply kept
an eye on the destination board. 'I grew up here. It's only
a question of reading the signs, anyway. You'd have been
fine by yourself.'

Nat would always be fine, she thought enviously. It

was impossible to imagine him lost or bewildered or unable to cope. It was nice of him to make her feel useful but he didn't really need her, did he?

It was only a five-minute walk to the Ashcrofts' house from the station. They made their way up a hill, along a quiet, leafy street with carefully-kept front gardens. To Prue, it felt very suburban after the bustling area where Cleo lived in Fulham, but she preferred it in many ways, and she thought Nat would appreciate the respite from the constant noise of traffic that was joined every couple of minutes by the roar of planes coming in to land at Heathrow.

She turned to say as much to Nat, but he was looking so withdrawn that the words died on her lips. He was walking with his head bent, his hands thrust into his pockets, and there was a bleakness about his expression that clutched at her heart.

'Are you thinking about the last time you were here?' she asked gently.

Nat threw her a quick, surprised glance. 'How did you know?'

'It's what I would be thinking, if it was me,' said Prue, imagining Nat as he had been then, arriving alone in a strange city after that long, disorientating flight, knowing that two tiny babies were now utterly dependent on him. Thinking about them and helping Laura's distraught parents cope with their grief, he could have had little time to mourn his brother properly himself.

She bit her lip, remembering how she had sat on the tube and envied Nat his calm competence. Nat would always be fine, hadn't she decided that? Well, maybe he would be, but that didn't mean that things were always easy for him. He had broad shoulders, but the last time he had walked along the road he must have had a lot to bear.

'This week's going to be awful for you,' she said, her grey eyes full of compassion. 'Having to pretend that you're happy when just being here must remind you of Ed and Laura and everything you went through last time. It seems all wrong to be going to all these parties Cleo's got lined up and drinking champagne and celebrating when they lost everything.'

Nat was touched and more than a little disconcerted by her concern. He couldn't remember the last time anyone had looked at him the way she was looking at him now, as if they really cared how he was feeling instead of waiting expectantly for him to solve their problems.

'It's true that I was remembering what it was like before,' he said, 'but life goes on. I do miss Ed—and Laura—but I've had time to get used to it now. It's not so bad this time.'

One of the reasons it wasn't so bad was that Prue was with him, Nat had been thinking, but he couldn't tell her that. He didn't want her thinking that he needed her or anything. *You'd have been fine by yourself.* Wasn't that what she had said when he had told her that he was glad she was with him? It was almost as if she had been warning him off getting too dependent on her.

Prue was still worrying about Nat and the run-up to the wedding. 'I should have thought about how difficult it's going to be for you this week,' she said remorsefully. 'I could explain to Cleo, if you like, and get you out of some of the parties.'

'No, don't do that,' said Nat. 'Ed always loved a party. I know he'd much rather we celebrated than cried. Besides, it's good not to have too much time to think, and it doesn't sound as if Cleo's going to give either of us much of that,' he added, trying to lighten the mood.

Even so, he fell silent as they neared the house, and Prue saw him take a breath and square his shoulders as they paused at the front gate.

She had a choice, she realised. She could say that she didn't want to be a nanny after all, that she'd changed her mind and would find some other way of getting back to Australia. She could walk away if she wanted to, but Nat couldn't. His brother's children needed him, and now that he was here there would be no turning back. Reaching out to push the bell, Nat must know that his life was about to change for good.

Prue slipped her hand into his, offering the only comfort she could. 'It'll be all right,' she promised him.

Nat's fingers tightened gratefully around hers, and as he looked down into her clear grey eyes he nodded slowly. 'Yes,' he said. 'I think it will now.'

CHAPTER SIX

WILLIAM and Daisy were awake. Prue and Nat could hear them bellowing at the top of their lungs as soon as they stepped into the house. Harry Ashcroft had looked decidedly harassed as he opened the door.

'I'm sorry about this,' he said apologetically when Nat had introduced Prue. He had to raise his voice to make himself heard. 'We were hoping that the twins would be settled before you arrived as it's impossible to concentrate when they're crying. Ruth's upstairs helping Eve change their nappies, but her arthritis is bad at the moment so she's a bit slow.'

'Why don't I go and give Eve a hand?' suggested Prue, seeing that Nat for once looked at a loss. 'That'll give the three of you a chance to talk, and Eve and I can bring William and Daisy down when they're ready.'

Nat looked at her so gratefully that she felt a warm glow deep inside her as she went up the stairs. Ruth Ashcroft was even more grateful when Prue appeared, to take over Daisy's nappy, but funnily enough the older woman's thanks didn't have nearly the same effect.

Choosing not to analyse just why that should be, Prue concentrated instead on William and Daisy. By the time the two babies had been changed and cuddled she was already in thrall to their tiny hands, their warm solid bodies and the serious little faces that could dissolve into enchanting smiles.

Both had a quiff of blonde hair and big brown eyes, but it was easy to tell the difference between them.

William was sturdier and more placid, while Daisy had a distinctly mischievous look about her. Prue cuddled William against her shoulder, wincing as his dimpled fingers clutched at her hair, and wondered how Nat was getting on downstairs.

'They're lovely babies,' she was able to tell him later as they walked back to the station.

'You were very good with them,' said Nat, remembering the blissful hush that had fallen soon after Prue had gone upstairs.

It hadn't been an easy conversation with Ruth and Harry, who were both still shattered by the tragedy. In the face of their overwhelming grief Nat had felt hopelessly inadequate, and he had found himself wishing that Prue had been there.

And then, as if she had known how much he needed her, the door had opened and she had come in, holding Daisy naturally on her hip, and he had felt a great weight roll off him. She had known just what to do and what to say. She had sat with Ruth and let her cry for her lost daughter while he and Harry, helpless to deal with the pent-up tears, had taken the babies out to the garden.

'We're so glad you're here,' Ruth had said with a tremulous smile when it had come to say goodbye. 'It makes such a difference having met you.'

Nat was very glad that Prue had been there too. Kathryn would have been charming to the Ashcrofts, but she wouldn't have known what to do with a crying baby or a grieving mother. Prue had.

'Thank you for coming,' he said stiltedly, and then admitted in a rush, 'I don't know what I would have done without you.'

Prue thought about the expression on Nat's face when she had gone down to the sitting room. It had obviously

been a difficult meeting for all of them, and it had no
doubt been sheer relief at the interruption that had made
him smile like that, but her heart had turned over at the
sight of him. She could still feel a strange tingling along
her veins.

Of course, it had probably been just the jet lag catching
up with her, she realised that now, but at the time her
reaction had taken her by surprise and she hoped that her
smile in return hadn't been too...too revealing. Quite
what it might have revealed, Prue wasn't sure. She just
knew that she felt ridiculously awkward and self-
conscious now.

She hugged her arms together as she walked, afraid
that if left to their own devices they might start reaching
towards him to offer a physical comfort that Nat certainly
wouldn't want. It must have been a traumatic meeting for
him, and at the very least an emotional occasion. The last
thing he needed was to suspect that she was crass enough
to be thinking about the way he had smiled or the feel
of his lips or the warm clasp of his fingers around hers
as they waited for Harry to open the door.

'I was just doing my job,' she said with would-be
lightness.

She wasn't looking at Nat, so she didn't see his face
close. 'Of course,' he agreed in a flat voice. 'Just doing
your job.'

'It will be easier tomorrow,' Prue assured him. 'The
first meeting was bound to be difficult, but now that's
over we can concentrate on William and Daisy.'

She wished they could have spent longer with the
babies, but there was still this evening to get through.
Cleo had invited their parents round for supper and she
and Nat would no doubt have to endure an in-depth in-

terrogation as to how they met and why and when and where they were planning to get married.

As it turned out, the evening went off better than Prue had anticipated. True, her mother was inclined to be suspicious of Nat, but he and her father seemed to get on well and they seemed to have brushed through the inevitable questions without raising too many eyebrows.

All in all, Prue decided the next day, it had gone pretty well, especially considering that she had spent the whole evening feeling jittery at the thought of climbing into bed next to Nat. In the event, even that hadn't been difficult. Exhaustion had simply got the better of nerves. Nat had tactfully let her go to bed first, and by the time he'd come into the room Prue had been sound asleep.

She hadn't woken until Nat had brought her a cup of tea this morning, and now it seemed perfectly natural to lie back against the pillows while he sat on the edge of the bed and drank his own tea. They chatted so comfortably that Prue's spirits rose.

She had simply been disorientated after the long flight yesterday. Why else would she have got herself into such a state about Nat and how it felt whenever he touched her? Prue sipped her tea and reflected that she must have been even more tired than she had thought. She had hardly given Ross a thought all day!

Now, she carefully built his picture in her mind. The hunky body. The blue eyes. The devastating smile. It seemed incredible to think that she had once or twice been on the verge of muddling him up with Nat.

No, everything would be fine now that she had had a good night's sleep, just as Nat had promised. No more embarrassment, no more awkwardness. They would simply get on with what they had come to do and when they went back to Australia, with any luck, Ross would be waiting for her.

They spent Tuesday with the twins in Wimbledon, and that evening had a quiet meal with Cleo and Alex. By the time she woke up on Wednesday morning Prue was feeling confident, even cocky, about her ability to keep up the pretence. All that fuss she had made, just because of a little jet lag!

In buoyant spirits, she waved Nat off to Wimbledon on his own and headed into town with her sister. She let Cleo bully her into buying not one but three new outfits, recklessly charging them to her credit card. She pretended to like the bridesmaid's dress that had been made for her, and chose a pair of shoes that she thought she would be able to stand in all day. They had coffee out, and Prue smiled and listened to Cleo's gossip and told herself that she really *was* enjoying herself.

It was just that the thought of Nat and the twins lingered distractingly at the back of her mind. She would drift off in the middle of one of Cleo's anecdotes, or pause in the act of pulling a top off the rail, and she would find herself wondering where the three of them were and what they were doing and how they were getting on without her.

Cleo waved a hand in front of her face. 'Prue! Have you been listening to a word I've said?'

'Sorry.' Prue recollected herself hastily and realised that she was standing in front of a cosmetic counter while Cleo tried to decide what colour lipstick she needed to go with her bridesmaid's dress. 'Um...you were thinking about the pink, weren't you?' she guessed wildly.

'No, Prue, I never even *mentioned* pink!' Cleo rolled her eyes. 'Honestly, I know you always used to be in a world of your own, but you were never as bad as you are now. Falling in love seems to have softened your brain!'

'I was only wondering what Nat and the twins were doing,' Prue said defensively.

Abandoning hope of getting a sensible opinion from her sister, Cleo selected a lipstick and handed it over to the assistant behind the counter. 'They'll be fine,' she said. 'Nat seems a capable type. I'm sure he doesn't need you hovering round him every second of the day.'

'No,' agreed Prue, and a wistful sigh escaped before she could stop herself.

It didn't escape Cleo, who subjected her to a shrewd blue stare. 'I hope you don't mind me saying this, Prue,' she said carefully as she turned away to sign the credit card slip, 'but how well do you actually know Nat?'

Prue was taken aback by the question. It was true that she and Nat hadn't spent that much time together. In fact, when she did a quick mental calculation, she worked out that it came to less than a week—but somehow it felt like much more than that.

Being with Nat, Prue told herself, was like putting on a pair of old slippers. Not wildly exciting, perhaps, but familiar, *comfortable*. Almost as if she had always known him: the way he moved, the way he spoke, the way he smiled.

The way he kissed?

Prue's heart stumbled as the thought slid insidiously into her head, and she frowned. She wasn't meant to be thinking about that kiss. That had been Monday, and things had been different then. Today Nat was just...a friend.

'I know him well enough,' she said shortly.

'Don't get me wrong,' said Cleo, misinterpreting her scowl. 'Nat's very nice. Even Dad liked him, and you

know how hard *he* is to please! It's just that you don't
seem that close,' she tried to explain her concern as they
headed towards the little brasserie she had chosen for
lunch.

Prue eyed her warily. 'What do you mean?'

'Most couples are a bit more affectionate with each
other,' Cleo pointed out. 'I've hardly seen you two touch
each other, and if it wasn't for the way I've seen you
look sometimes I'd wonder how well you knew each
other. That's why I asked,' she admitted.

So much for thinking that she and Nat had been convincing! Prue was dismayed at her sister's assessment.
'We're sharing a bed, aren't we?' she said, opting for
attack as a better form of defence.

'Oh, sex!' Cleo waved her hand dismissively. 'I'm sure
you have a great physical relationship, but you need more
than that if you're going to get married, Prue. You need
to be comfortable with each other when you're not in bed
as well as when you are. I just get the feeling that you
and Nat *aren't*. It's as if you're really aware of each other
but don't dare show it.'

Prue moistened her lips. Cleo was getting a little too
close to the truth for comfort. 'Nat's not very demonstrative in public, but that's just the way he is,' she managed.

'I hope it's enough for you,' said Cleo dubiously. 'I
know it's not really any of my business, but Mum and I
are both worried. You've always had this dream about
the outback, and we're afraid that you're getting carried
away by the romance of it all.'

She stopped in the middle of the pavement and caught
hold of Prue's arm, her blue eyes unusually serious. 'We
don't want to spoil anything for you, Prue, but you're
talking about marrying a man you don't seem that com-

fortable with, taking on two small children and going to live in the middle of nowhere. Are you sure you know what you're doing?'

Prue looked back into her sister's face. Cleo was practically shouting over the relentless sound of a drill which was drowning out the noise of all the idling engines as the traffic stalled, bumper to bumper both ways, belching out exhaust fumes. Trapped between the tall buildings, the fumes hung stubbornly in the muggy air, making her eyes sting. All around them office workers, heading out to get a sandwich for lunch, jostled impatiently through the crowds.

She didn't even need to close her eyes to picture the verandah at Mack River, with its shady garden blending into the scrubby trees and the river gums beyond. Prue could see it all so clearly. Nat in one of the chairs, with a baby standing on his lap—Daisy, perhaps—exploring his face with inquisitive little fingers, patting his nose, making him laugh. The shrieks and whistles of the birds. The smell of the bush. The warm weight of William in her arms as she—

Prue's imagination jolted to a sickening halt. No, that wasn't right!

Hastily, she rewound the scene and mentally replaced it with the kitchen at Cowen Creek, with Ross, tall and handsome, taking off his hat with a smile and reaching for her.

That was what she wanted, wasn't it? Her grey gaze refocused on Cleo's concerned face. 'I know just what I'm doing,' she said, although she didn't sound quite as sure as she would have liked.

'You can wear that dress you bought,' said Cleo that evening, loading Prue up with shopping bags and pushing her towards the bedroom. 'You know what Sabrina's like! Her parties are always smart and you need to look the part.'

What part? Prue wondered as she stood under the shower. She was having trouble remembering what part she was playing and what she wasn't.

She wished they didn't have to go out. She had hardly seen Nat. He hadn't returned by the time they'd got back to the flat and when he had come in, half an hour or so later, he seemed to have drawn into himself.

Conscious of her sister's interested gaze, Prue had gone to welcome him with a quick kiss. She had been hoping that Cleo wouldn't notice that she had only dared to kiss his cheek, but even that had taken Nat by surprise and he had tensed as she reached up to press her lips against the corner of his mouth.

He had practically flinched, Prue remembered miserably. It was hard to believe that she had started the day in such good spirits. Somewhere along the line her conviction that she and Nat could spend the next month as friends had deflated and she was left with the uneasy feeling that things just weren't going to be that easy after all.

She had had no chance to tell Nat about Cleo's suspicions. They hadn't had a moment alone, and she had been reduced to asking him politely about his day. He had spent most of it with Eve, he'd said, learning as much as he could about the twins' routine and drawing up a list of things he would need to buy before they came to stay.

'Ruth and Harry were both disappointed you weren't with me,' Nat told Prue, omitting to add that he had missed her much more than they had.

It had been a long day. Reluctant to admit how often

he'd found himself wishing that Prue was with him or how many times he had turned to say something to her only to remember that she wasn't there, Nat blamed his tiredness. He hadn't slept well again. Prue had been dead to the world when he'd got into bed, but he had found it harder to relax when she was so tantalisingly close.

The street light outside the window threw a weirdly orange glow onto the ceiling, casting enough light to see her face as a pale blur against the pillow and her bare arm curled across her chest. Nat had been able to smell her shampoo, a clean fresh fragrance with a faint hint of something he hadn't quite been able to identify. Herbs? Almonds? Coconut?

Without thinking, he had moved closer and lifted a lock of her hair to his face, rubbing its softness between his fingers before he'd realised just what he was doing and dropped it as if it had bitten him.

Moving firmly back to his side of the bed, Nat had set his jaw and stared up at the ceiling. Outside, he had heard the sound of traffic punctuated by a distant siren. A couple had gone by, arguing, and somehow, somewhere there had been the distinctive noise of a washing machine entering its spin cycle.

Who would do their washing in the middle of the night? Nat had wondered, half convinced that he was imagining it. He had waited for the noise to stop, but it never had. He'd heard footsteps and banging doors, cars being parked or driven away. A neighbour had had music playing. Revellers had headed home from the pub right underneath the bedroom window, unable to tell how loud their voices sounded in the night air. Did no one in London ever sleep?

Nat's eyes had strayed over to Prue, breathing quietly

beside him, and he had sighed. It looked like being a very long week.

And now they had a party to get through. Intent on organising everyone, Cleo had allowed him to shower and change and then he had been sent to wait with Alex in the sitting room while the girls did whatever it was girls did when they got ready to go out.

Nat was reassured to discover that Alex had no clearer idea than he did. Over a beer, they speculated as to what was going on in the next room, and they were getting on better than either of them had expected when the door opened and a shrinking Prue was pushed into the room.

'There!' said Cleo triumphantly. 'Doesn't she look beautiful?'

Nat hardly heard her. Pole-axed by the sight of Prue, he rose unthinkingly to his feet, perhaps hoping that it would be easier to breathe upright. He couldn't take his eyes off her. Her hair was a soft cloud, framing her pale, pointed face, and the huge grey eyes were apprehensive, sliding nervously away from his.

She was wearing a short dress that stopped just above her knees. It was made of some silvery material that glimmered beneath a layer of grey chiffon and clung lovingly to the curves of her body. Dry-mouthed, Nat let his gaze travel down from the slender knees to where her bare feet were encased in delicate silver sandals. He had never seen Prue's legs before, he realised irrelevantly. He had had no idea that she could look so...so...

'Well?' demanded Cleo. 'What do you think?'

Nat swallowed the constriction in his throat. 'You look very nice,' he said, and saw by the brittleness of Prue's smile how inadequate a compliment it had been.

'Very nice? Is that all you can say?' Cleo didn't bother to hide her disgust. 'Some fiancé *you* are!'

She turned to Prue. 'Don't listen to Nat,' she admonished her. 'You look fantastic. The trouble with you, Prue, is that you don't *try*. You could be beautiful, but because you never make the effort nobody ever notices and you just—'

'I notice.' Nat's quiet voice cut across Cleo's affectionate scolding, and something in his face made her stop in mid-sentence.

Ignoring Cleo and Alex, Nat went over to Prue and ran a gentle finger down her cheek. 'I notice you,' he said softly. 'I notice everything about you.'

Prue stared up into his face, mesmerised by the expression in his eyes. She could feel her blood beating and the nerves just below her skin began to tingle as he smoothed the hair tenderly away from her forehead so that he could hold her face between his palms.

'I notice the way the light catches your hair,' he told her, and the two of them might have been alone in the room—in the world. 'I notice your cheekbones and your eyes and the way you smile. You don't need a new dress for me to notice how beautiful you are.'

Prue was giddy and trembling inside. She felt as if she was standing on the brink of a bottomless chasm of feeling, and Nat's hands were all that prevented her from tumbling forwards and down. Her heart was slamming so painfully against her ribs that she was afraid she might actually pass out.

She opened her mouth, but no sound came out and she had no idea what she would have said. It didn't matter anyway, because the next moment Nat's mouth came down on hers and the room, Cleo, Alex, the need to think or find something to say, all evaporated. There was only the warm persuasion of his lips and the flame inside her that leapt to respond.

Prue let out a shivery sigh of release as Nat's hands left her face and his arms went round her, gathering her close against his hard body. Her bones were melting, dissolving in a golden rush of pleasure, and she clung to him with a kind of desperation, afraid of where it might take her, not wanting to know where the kiss might end, not wanting it to end at all.

That's enough, Nat's brain instructed him. Let her go.

Nat knew that he should, but she tasted so sweet and she felt so good in his arms that he couldn't, not yet.

Let her go, his brain insisted as its control slipped alarmingly. *Let her go!*

Slowly, reluctantly, Nat obeyed. He lifted his head and loosened his hold, but he still kept one arm around her. That was allowed, surely?

'That's a bit more like it!' Cleo was surveying them with a satisfied air. 'We were beginning to wonder if you two were in love at all, but I have to say that I'm convinced!'

Alex laughed. 'Either that, or they're very good actors!' he said.

His words splintered Prue's daze of enchantment and she stiffened. *Acting.* That was all it had been. Cheeks burning, she jerked herself out of the circle of Nat's arm.

'Don't be silly, Alex,' she said, and her voice was so husky that she had to clear her throat. She couldn't look at Nat. 'If we're going to this party, hadn't we better go?'

Prue had never thought that she would be glad to be going to one of Sabrina's parties, but the alternative would have been an intimate meal with just the four of them. She would have had to sit next to Nat under Cleo's disconcertingly sharp gaze and try to behave normally. How could she have done that when she was shaken and still shocked by how easily she had abandoned herself to his kiss, when her body was still thumping and her mind awhirl with memory?

At least the party would be a distraction for all of them, and with any luck it would give her a chance to calm down a bit. Nat had been so *convincing*. He had looked down into her eyes and kissed her as if he really loved her. No wonder Cleo had believed him. She had almost believed him herself.

And she had been convincing as well, Prue remembered uneasily. Too convincing. She had just stood there, staring dazedly up into his face as if there was no one else in the world. The very model of a besotted fiancée!

Prue cringed as she sat in the taxi Alex had waved down. Anyone would have thought that she was head over heels in love with Nat, which was ridiculous, of course. She wasn't in love with him. She couldn't be.

She hardly knew him, Prue reminded herself with an edge of desperation. You couldn't fall in love with someone when you had barely known them a week...could you?

Of course, she had fallen in love with Ross at first sight, but that had been different. That had been wild and romantic. Perfect, in fact, Prue told herself. She didn't feel that for Nat at all.

He was familiar to her in a way that Ross had never been. She had always been too dazzled by Ross's looks or too preoccupied by the churning sensation in her stomach whenever he was near to relax and get to know what made him tick. Nat didn't overwhelm her in the same way, but that wasn't the same as falling in love, was it? It was just that the better she knew him, the more she appreciated why a girl as reputedly stunning as Kathryn might want to marry him and the less she understood why Kathryn had let him go.

Sabrina was a glamorous redhead with a private trust
fund which she drew on for the lavish parties she loved.
She always made Prue feel dowdy and dull, but Prue had
to admit that Sabrina was incredibly generous, even if
she was a bit over the top. She swept down on them as
they arrived, kissed them all extravagantly, and promptly
annexed Nat.

'So you're Prue's cowboy!' she cried. 'Come with me,
everyone's *dying* to meet you!'

To Prue's consternation, Nat seemed amused rather
than overpowered by Sabrina, and he let himself be borne
off without so much as a backward glance. Craning her
neck to keep the two of them in view, she saw Sabrina
tuck her hand cosily into his arm and Nat smile down at
her.

Kathryn was a redhead too, Prue remembered with a
cold trickle down her spine. Perhaps Sabrina reminded
him of his first love? From what he and Ross had told
her, Sabrina and Kathryn were not unalike.

Prue tried to shrug off the thought. If Nat liked that
rather flashy kind of beauty, there was nothing she could
do about it. She just hoped he didn't think he would ever
get Sabrina to the outback, she thought sourly. Sabrina
felt that she was roughing it if she stepped out of
Knightsbridge.

The party was just as bad as Prue had feared. The room
was hot and crowded, and everyone was shouting at the
tops of their voices to make themselves heard over the
band in the corner. She had met most of Cleo's friends
over the years, so there was no shortage of people to talk
to, but most of them only wanted to ask her about Nat.
Prue was soon sick of jokes about kangaroos and boo-
merangs and Crocodile Dundee. Paul Hogan had a lot to
answer for, she decided wearily.

She kept losing sight of Nat. Sabrina was dragging him round the room like a prize exhibit—look what Prue brought back from Australia!—and whenever she did catch a glimpse of him he was surrounded by admiring girls, all running their hands through their hair and sending him flirty little glances under their lashes.

Heaven only knew what they saw in him, thought Prue crossly. It couldn't be for his looks, that was for sure, and it wasn't as if he was making any effort to charm them either. He was just standing there, as cool and contained as ever, listening courteously to their inanities and keeping his inevitable opinion to himself.

It must just be because he was different, she decided. Next to Nat, the other men in the room looked somehow pale and insubstantial. His admiring audience was simply avid for anything new. If Nat didn't watch out, he would become a craze.

Prue smiled wryly at the idea. It was ironic that Nat, the calmest and least crazy man she had ever met, should be the object of such feverish attention. Those girls hanging on his every word didn't know Nat. They didn't know what he was really like or where he really belonged.

Unbidden, a picture of Mack River sprang into her mind, and she remembered how they had ridden among the trees, how quiet it had been. The silence had beaten down around them, broken only by the gentle whicker of the horses and the jingle of their bits as they shook their manes occasionally against the flies.

Prue could still smell the hot, dry air and the dried leaves that had been crushed under the horses' hooves. She could practically *feel* the reins in her hand. So vivid was the memory that she could almost believe that if she turned her head Nat would be there by her side, looking utterly at home, his hat tilted over his eyes and his mouth set in that cool, quiet line that snarled her senses whenever she looked at it.

The longing to be there was suddenly so intense that Prue closed her eyes, screwing them shut as if against a pain. When she opened them again Nat was in front of her, looking down at her with a hard, anxious expression in his eyes, but the trees and the horses and the diamond-bright light had all gone and she felt a wave of bitter disappointment wash over her.

Nat frowned. 'Are you all right?'

Prue couldn't look at him. She felt sick, shaken, perilously close to tears. 'I'm fine,' she muttered.

'I thought you were about to faint.'

'I'm *fine*.'

'We can go if you want,' Nat offered.

All Prue wanted was to be at Mack River or, failing that, in a dark room where she could lock herself in for a good cry. But she couldn't do that because then he would want to know what the matter was, and how could she tell him when she didn't know herself?

She lifted her chin. 'I'd hate to tear you away when you're having such a good time,' she snapped. 'Oh, look, there's Sabrina! She'll be coming to find out what you're doing wasting your time talking to me. I mean, I'm only your fiancée!'

Too late, Prue heard the jealous note in her voice, and her brief spurt of anger at his obtuseness died. 'Pretend fiancée, anyway,' she muttered.

'Prue—' Nat began, but before he could finish Sabrina was bearing down on them.

'There you are, Prue! Where have you been hiding? Everyone's been wondering what happened to you. I'd keep an eye on Nat if I were you,' she added. 'We're all smitten!'

She leant confidentially closer. 'Congratulations!' she said in a stage whisper. 'That strong, silent look is to *die* for! Not that you've any need to be jealous,' she went on with a smile. 'Nat's been watching you all evening! I don't know what you did a minute ago, but he walked off in the middle of a conversation. Didn't say anything, just headed straight for you!' she said enviously. 'You lucky thing!'

'Sabrina!' said Nat quickly and held out his hand. 'It was nice to meet you.'

'Oh, but you're not going *already*?' Sabrina pouted. 'The party's only just beginning.'

'We're very tired,' said Nat, taking Prue's hand in a firm clasp. 'We only arrived a couple of days ago and you know what jet lag is like...'

'We want to be fresh for the wedding,' Prue put in, forcing a smile and trying to ignore the feel of Nat's fingers around hers.

Sabrina was obviously disappointed. 'I suppose you just want to be on your own,' she said a shade sulkily, and then recovered to smile her brilliant smile. 'Oh, well, I can't blame you! Cleo and Alex will be here to the bitter end, so you'll have the flat to yourselves,' she promised with a roguish wink.

Insisting on accompanying them to the door, she waved them off into the night. 'See you at the wedding!' she said.

CHAPTER SEVEN

IT WAS a relief to get out of the crowded house. Prue took a deep breath of night air as they walked down the steps.

Nat was holding her hand, but the moment Sabrina closed the door on them he gave it back to her like a parcel. Without the clasp of his fingers it felt cold and empty at the end of her arm, and Prue didn't know what to do with it. She tried it in various positions before folding her arms and tucking it out of sight at her waist as she pretended to look for a taxi.

'We might as well walk,' she suggested in a creditably cool voice when no yellow light appeared. 'It's not that far.'

They walked without touching through the summer night. To Nat, London seemed almost as busy by night as during the day. Plenty of shops were still open, and drinkers spilled out of the pubs to stand on the pavement in cheerful groups. The traffic continued to growl along the roads and, once, a police car zipped past, blue light flashing and siren whooping. Nat felt a long way from Mathison.

In spite of the noise and activity around them it seemed, to Prue, that the two of them were sealed off from it all, trapped in a bubble of constrained silence where there was nothing to keep the memory of the kiss they had shared at bay. It shimmered between them, unavoidable, unforgettable, making it impossible to think about anything else.

'Thank you for earlier,' said Prue awkwardly at last, unable to bear the tension any longer.

'What for?'

For kissing me. That was what she wanted to say, but her nerve failed her at the last minute. 'For saying what you did,' she said instead.

She felt Nat's quick glance. 'Don't mention it,' he said in a colourless voice.

Prue wished that she *hadn't* mentioned it, but she couldn't just leave it there. She forced a smile and tried to speak lightly. 'Did Cleo have a word with you too?'

'Cleo?' Nat sounded surprised. 'No. What about?'

'She's worried that we're not affectionate enough with each other.' Prue glanced at him. 'I assumed that she'd had a go at you too while I was in the bath.'

So that was why she had responded so willingly to his kiss. Nat was conscious of a sinking feeling in his stomach. She had just been trying to convince her sister that they really were engaged. Well, what had he expected? Had he really thought that there could have been any other reason for her to melt into his arms like that?

He watched a double-decker bus go past. 'I gathered Cleo had some doubts,' he said carefully, not quite lying. If Prue had a good excuse for kissing him so sweetly, he might as well pretend that he had approached the matter in a similarly cold-blooded spirit.

There was a pause.

'At least she's convinced now,' said Prue with a laugh that didn't quite come off.

'Yes, she is.'

Of course Cleo was convinced. Who wouldn't have been? The very air seemed to be mocking them, twanging with the memory of how they had held each other and kissed, not like two people pretending to be in love but like lovers.

Silence fell once more, awkward and uncomfortable. Prue was very conscious of the sound of her heels on the pavement. A fuzzy moon hung in the sky above the flashing lights of the planes still coming in to land at Heathrow, and the air was warm and thick, like soup, and alive with the night scent of the flowers crammed into windowboxes along the street. The streets were lined with parked cars, red lights winking on their dashboards to show that they were alarmed. To Prue they seemed to be blinking the same warning.

Be careful.

Don't make a fool of yourself.

Remember Kathryn.

Remember *Ross*.

Forget how he kissed you. It was just for show.

Hugging her arms to her, she kept her head down and concentrated on not walking on the cracks in the pavement.

'What are you doing?' asked Nat after he had been watching her careful steps for a while.

'I'm avoiding the bears.'

She saw that the reference meant nothing to him. Why should it? There were no pavements at Mack River.

'It's just a silly superstition,' she said, blushing. She pointed down at the paving-stones. 'It's supposed to be unlucky to tread on the lines, that's all. If you can keep your feet in the squares, you can make your wishes come true.'

Nat stopped, his hands in his pockets as he looked at her. 'What were you wishing for?' he asked.

What *did* she want? Prue felt as if she had walked smack into a wall in the dark and she took a step back, inadvertently stepping on a crack after all. She had grown so used to dreaming about Ross that it was a shock to realise that for the first time since she had met him his face didn't immediately spring to mind. She didn't *know* what she had been wishing for, Prue realised. The only thing she knew was that she felt confused and uncertain, and she didn't like it.

'Oh, you know,' she said uncomfortably.

Of course he knew, thought Nat bitterly. Prue had never made any secret of how she felt about Ross. It had been stupid to even ask.

'Yes, I know,' he said, and walked on down the dark street.

The flat felt very empty when they got in, and there was nothing to do but go to bed. Prue longed for the exhaustion that had made it all so simple last night, when she had been too tired to be embarrassed, but now she managed to feel weary and wide awake at the same time.

It was ridiculous to feel nervous, she knew. They had shared a bed perfectly easily before, and there was no reason why they shouldn't do the same again, but it didn't stop her stomach looping alarmingly as she changed in the bathroom. Pulling on her nightdress, Prue felt the coolness of the cotton against her skin and wished she could feel that cool inside.

She chewed her lip as she regarded her reflection in the bathroom mirror. It was a perfectly plain nightdress, falling from narrow straps to her calves, and although there was nothing glamorous or seductive about it she was conscious of her naked body beneath the thin material in a way she had never been in the past. The soft, fine cotton was all that would be between her and Nat when they were lying together in the dark.

Stop it! Stop it! Prue squeezed her eyes shut. She was

tired; Nat was tired. They would lie next to each other
and they would sleep, and absolutely nothing else would
happen. All she had to do was relax.

Relaxing, though, was easier said than done. The bed
seemed to have shrunk since the night before and Prue
was agonisingly aware of Nat beside her, very solid, very
close. He lay so still that she was afraid to toss and turn
in case she disturbed him, and had to content herself with
shifting cautiously on to one side and then the other. And
then back again. And again.

She was hot, then cold. Staring at the curtains, Prue
let out a long sigh. They would have been better off staying at the party. She was never going to be able to sleep!

But as she listened to Nat's slow, steady breathing, her
tension did in the end evaporate and she began gradually,
very gradually, to relax. She must have dropped off at
last, because the next thing Prue knew there was something heavy lying across her. Drifting on the edge of
sleep, she let her fingers explore it questioningly.

Nat's hand. Nat's arm. They were lying like spoons,
she realised, in the dream-like state where the answer
seemed obvious and somehow right. She was on her side,
and she could feel the length of his hard body curled
against her back. His face was half buried in her hair,
and his slow breath was a shivery caress against her bare
shoulder.

Behind her, Nat stirred, and Prue lay very still, her eyes
closed. Mumbling something she couldn't catch, he
pressed a warm kiss into her neck and sank back into
sleep.

Prue's eyes had flown open at the touch of his mouth
and she was suddenly wide awake, her skin tingling
where his lips had been. She let out a breath very carefully, without moving. It had been a reflex action on

Nat's part, that much was obvious. That mumble…had it been Kathryn's name? It could have been, but then it could have been anything—except her own name. He definitely hadn't said 'Prue'. He hadn't meant to kiss *her*.

A tiny sigh escaped Prue. She ought to disentangle herself from Nat and move away to her own side of the bed. But there was hardly any room, and if she pushed *him* away he might wake up. It wasn't that she wanted Nat to kiss her again—of course not—but she was comfortable and sleepy and there was no point in making a big deal out of something Nat hadn't even known he was doing. Prue's lashes closed. She might as well stay right where she was.

The sound of frantic barking greeted them as Cleo pushed open the gate and they walked up to the house together. 'Angus,' sighed Prue to Nat. 'Mum's dog. He's completely out of control.'

They had spent most of the day with William and Daisy, and the two babies had been so endearing that Prue hadn't wanted to leave them. Once or twice, when she looked at Nat, she had felt a peculiar sensation in her neck and she had put a hand unthinkingly to where it tingled.

She had a vague memory of waking in the night, curled up with him, his lips on her skin, but in the clear light of day Prue was more than half inclined to dismiss it as a dream. When she had woken that morning Nat had been nowhere near her. Still, like some vivid dreams, the impression had been hard to shake off, and it had left her acutely aware of him all day, as if all her senses had been set on high alert as far as he was concerned.

Her mother opened the door in response to Cleo's imperative ring on the doorbell and immediately a small terrier rushed out, wagging his tail and barking furiously. Thoroughly over-excited at the mixture of familiar and unfamiliar legs, he ran around in circles, lifted his leg on the nearest plant and completely ignored the family's attempts to quieten him.

'We'll just have to wait for him to calm down, I'm afraid,' Prue's mother apologised. 'Oh, do shut *up*, Angus!' she shouted without any expectation of being obeyed.

Nat looked down at the little dog, who was up on his hind legs and yapping hysterically for attention. 'Quiet!' he ordered, and to the utter amazement of everyone, Angus stopped in mid-yap.

'Now, sit!'

Responding to the quiet authority in his voice, Angus sank down onto his haunches and flattened his ears placatingly.

They all gaped at Nat and then at the dog, who was wagging his tail tentatively as he waited for his obedience to be acknowledged. Nat crouched down and fondled Angus's ears. 'Good dog,' he said.

Lucky Angus, thought Prue involuntarily as the others all continued to stare at Nat as if he had performed some kind of miracle.

'*Well!*' Her mother was obviously rapidly revising her estimate of Nat as a potential son-in-law. 'I've never seen him do that before! I'm impressed! Come in, Nat, and meet Marisa.'

Prue was left with Cleo and Alex to follow behind and close the door.

'Nat's well in now,' Cleo murmured in Prue's ear. 'Mum will elevate him to star status if he can handle Angus! If he can do that, he can do anything. Nat's a handy person to have around, isn't he?' she went on, eyeing Nat speculatively as he was ushered into the sitting room, Angus trotting angelically at his heels. 'Did you know he fixed the dripping tap in the bathroom, and that window I could never open? He didn't say a word. Alex would have made a huge fuss about how macho he was being, but Nat just went off and did it!'

Cleo took Prue's arm and smiled conspiratorially. 'You know, I'm beginning to see what you mean about him being attractive,' she confided. 'I noticed it at the party last night. Nat grows on you, doesn't he? And he's got a wonderful smile.'

'I know,' said Prue, who felt hollow at the very thought of it. She didn't need Cleo to remind her how Nat smiled. Right now, she would much rather that she could forget.

'Auntie Prue! Auntie Prue!' Her small niece and nephew came tumbling down the stairs to meet her, barely restrained by their father who had been bathing them.

Prue had spent a lot of time with Ben and Katie before she went to Australia and she was firmly established as their favourite aunt. Bending down to open her arms, she laughed as they hurtled into her. Delighted to see them, and secretly glad of the distraction, she let them clamber exuberantly over her before picking Katie up and carrying her into the sitting room, six-year-old Ben hanging from other hand.

Nat, cornered by Prue's elder sister and her husband, looked up in relief as Prue came in, a small child clinging to her neck and another tugging at her hand. Her hair was all over the place, but her silvery eyes were alight with laughter and Nat's heart turned over.

'Look what they've done to you!' Marisa tutted as she kissed Prue and pushed the tumbled curls back into some semblance of order, and Nat found his hands itching to slap her hands away so that he could do it himself.

'Children, this is Nat,' Marisa went on. 'He's going to marry Auntie Prue.'

She smiled apologetically at Nat. 'They're a bit shy with strangers,' she told him, but Ben was already taking the hand Nat held gravely out to him.

'Why are you going to marry Auntie Prue?' he asked.

Prue gave a tiny gasp that was half-laugh, half-embarrassment, but Nat didn't even hesitate. 'Because I'm in love with her,' he told the little boy.

'Why?'

Nat glanced up at Prue, who was clutching Katie to her, the grey eyes a mixture of appeal and apology. 'I think you might need to be a bit older to understand,' he said.

Ben considered this. 'What do you have to do to be in love with someone?' he asked, interested, and Nat's mouth twitched.

'You don't have to do anything,' he answered seriously, although all the others were laughing, except Prue, who just looked agonised. 'You just are.'

'But *why*?'

His father, Phil, rescued Nat. 'You have to kiss girls when you're in love with them,' he said, teasing. 'You wouldn't want to do that, would you, Ben?'

'No!' Appalled, Ben screwed up his face. He had reached the stage where he would tolerate being kissed by his mother in private, but that was about it. 'Yuk!'

Even Prue couldn't help laughing then. 'Sorry, Ben! I shouldn't have kissed you just now. I'd forgotten that you would have grown up since I've been away.'

'I don't mind *you*,' said Ben generously. 'I like it when you kiss me. You smell nice.'

Nat knew exactly what he meant. He straightened. 'There you are,' he said to Ben, but his eyes were on Prue. 'I feel like that too. That's why I want to marry her.'

Ridiculously, Prue blushed, which only made her wretched family laugh harder.

'Oh.' Ignoring the adults' mystifying behaviour, Ben nodded sagely. He smiled up at Nat. 'Do you want to see my super-blaster?'

'No, Ben, not now,' Marisa put in hurriedly. 'It's time for bed.'

A stormy look gathered on Ben's face, and a mighty tantrum was only averted when Nat and Prue agreed to go up and read the two children a bedtime story. 'But only if you're good now!' their mother said sternly.

Later, Prue sat with Katie on her lap, and rested her cheek on the soft curls. She was trying to read about Goldilocks, but she kept stumbling over the simplest words. She couldn't seem to focus on the page. It was something to do with Nat, sitting opposite her on the bed that had once been hers, reading to Ben in the deep, slow voice that seemed to reverberate up and down her spine. It wasn't just a sound, it was a physical sensation as real as if he was smoothing a warm hand over her bare back.

'Cold?' Feeling her aunt shiver, Katie twisted round and looked up at Prue in concern.

'No, not cold.' Prue forced a smile and cleared her throat. '"And then Baby Bear said…"'

The evening seemed to last for ever. When Ben and Katie had been tucked up, they had champagne and drank a toast to Cleo and Alex, who kissed blissfully. Prue carefully avoided Nat's eye until, to her horror, she realised that Cleo was proposing another toast.

'I think we should drink to Prue and Nat, too,' she said, gesturing to Alex to refill all their glasses.

'Oh, no…' stuttered Prue, caught unawares. 'I mean, this is *your* evening, Cleo.'

'I don't mind sharing it with you,' said Cleo gaily. 'Don't worry, I'll have Saturday all to myself, but we need to celebrate your engagement properly too.'

'I agree.' Prue's father unexpectedly entered the discussion. 'We're all very happy for you, darling,' he said, kissing her, and then turned to shake Nat's hand. 'This seems a good time to welcome you to the family while we're all here. Prue's very precious to us,' he added, a faint hint of warning in his voice. 'We hope you'll look after her for us.'

Returning his grip, Nat looked at Prue. 'I will,' he promised.

'To Prue and Nat!'

As her family raised their glasses, Nat met Prue's anguished grey gaze and he set his jaw at her obvious distaste at the idea that he might have to kiss her again. With the others beaming expectantly around them, he didn't see that they had much choice, but he tried to spare her by lifting her hand and kissing it.

It wasn't enough. They were all still waiting, and Nat could see Cleo's fine brows already beginning to rise at his hesitation. Pulling Prue towards him, he bent his head and touched his lips to her mouth. He would make it quick.

The floor tilted beneath Prue's feet as his mouth came down on hers. It was just like it had been the night before, she realised with a mixture of elation and despair. The same jolt of excitement, the same treacherous urge to forget this pretence they were committed to and let herself believe that it was real.

She had sensed Nat's hesitation too. She knew why he was kissing her, and that it only needed to be brief, but somehow their lips caught and clung and wouldn't let go, and before she knew where she was she was kissing him back and her bones were dissolving into honey, and she was pierced by a sweetness so intense that tears stung and shimmered in her eyes when he at last let her go.

And that was just the beginning. They had more champagne, and then they had to sit down to a three-course meal that her mother had spent days preparing. Prue pushed her food around her plate. She didn't think she could eat.

She worried that she might be running a fever. There was a jittery sensation under her skin and she kept going hot and cold. She felt fragile, as if the slightest touch would shatter her into a million pieces.

And she couldn't keep her eyes off Nat. She was fascinated by his hands, by the way they held his fork or lifted his glass, by how strong and brown they looked against the pale tablecloth, and she thought about the feel of his fingers against her face, about the warm press of lips against her neck last night, and she shivered again. Had she dreamt it? *Had* she?

Prue drank her wine with a kind of desperation, latching onto fragments of the conversation swirling around her but unable to make any sense of it. All she could think about was Nat's calm, quiet presence opposite. She tried not to stare at him, and her gaze skittered frantically around the table in search of something else to look at, but whenever she managed to fix it on the pepper mill or the dribble of wax down the side of a candle it would be tugged back by the gleam of Nat's slow smile.

By the tilt of his head.

By his throat as he swallowed.

There was a constriction around Prue's heart, as if all the air had evaporated from her lungs. She wanted to reach across the table and uncurl his fingers from the glass he held. She wanted to take his hand and pull him out of the room.

She wanted Nat to press her against the wall outside and to kiss her again. She wanted to wind her arms around him and burrow into the steely strength of his body, to tug the shirt from his trousers so that she could run her hands over his back, feeling his muscles flex beneath her fingers.

Oh, and she wanted him to smile against her throat, to peel off her clothes, to kiss his—

'Prue?'

Prue took a sharp, startled breath, as if someone had dashed a bucket of cold water in her face. 'S-sorry…what?' she gasped.

Her family regarded her with amusement. 'You've hardly eaten a thing,' her mother said reprovingly. 'Is something wrong?'

'I'm just…not hungry.'

'Poor old Prue! You *have* got it bad!' said Cleo, patting her sister's hand indulgently. 'I've never seen you in love like this before!'

In love.

It was all Prue could do not to clap her hands to her mouth. She stared wide-eyed at Cleo, who laughed.

'Well, don't look so appalled!' she teased. 'You're engaged to Nat. You're allowed to be in love with him!'

But she wasn't.

She couldn't have fallen in love with Nat, she told herself frantically. It was just…

Just what? Just the need to be with him? Just the want-

ing to touch him? Just the longing to spend the rest of
her life with him?

What if Nat had guessed? Prue thought in panic. Her
sisters seemed to think her expression was utterly trans-
parent. What if he too had been sitting there, his heart
sinking as he realised what a fool she was making of
herself?

They were all waiting for her to say something. Prue
opened her mouth, but no words came out, and in spite
of herself her eyes lifted to Nat's. They held an indeci-
pherable expression, but he smiled reassuringly at her and
she relaxed slightly. Surely he wouldn't have smiled if
he had guessed the truth? He would have curled his lip
in disgust or turned away, wondering how to remind her
about Kathryn. He wouldn't have *smiled*.

Marisa had been watching the exchange of looks across
the table. 'I think you'd better have the wedding as soon
as possible,' she said drily, and Prue's head jerked round.
'*Marisa…*'

'Well, why not?' Her mother picked up on the idea.
'There's no reason why you shouldn't get married before
you go back to Australia, is there?'

'Good idea.' It was Cleo's turn to chime in. 'Just wait
until Alex and I get back from our honeymoon!'

Prue stared at her. Only two days ago she and her
mother had been shaking their heads over the whole idea
of her marrying Nat, and now here they were, pushing
her into it as soon as possible. And all because Angus
had sat when Nat told him to!

'It's too soon,' she said, managing a brittle smile.

'But you seem so right together! Why wait?'

Because Nat's in love with another woman, Prue
wanted to shout. She mumbled something about William
and Daisy, but Cleo was having none of it.

'You getting married won't make any difference to them,' she pointed out. 'If anything, it'll be better for them. Give them a nice stable background, that kind of thing.'

'Yes, and I'll happily look after them if you want to have a honeymoon,' offered Marisa. 'Katie and Ben would love having them to stay.'

Prue wished they would both shut up. 'We don't *want*—'she began loudly, at the end of her tether.

'We want to get married in Australia,' Nat cut across her before she could blurt out the truth. His voice was quiet, but Cleo and Marisa subsided instantly. 'Don't we, Prue?' he added, knowing that was what she really wanted. She just didn't want to marry him.

Prue managed a nod, not looking at him. Getting married in Australia was what Nat wanted, after all. He just didn't want to marry her. He wanted Kathryn, beautiful Kathryn, who belonged with him and who everyone knew was meant to be with him.

'Oh, well.' Her mother and sisters were disappointed but not downcast. 'We'll just have to come out to Australia, then.'

Prue looked at them in consternation. 'We wouldn't expect that,' she tried. 'It's such a long way.'

'Nonsense!' Her mother disposed of that objection without any trouble. 'Of course we're coming to your wedding.'

'Besides, it's a good excuse for a holiday,' said Marisa to Prue's amazement. Marisa? In *Australia*? She couldn't picture it.

'I don't think—'

Cleo went on the attack. 'What's the matter?' she demanded. 'Don't you want us to come?'

'It's not—'

'Of course we want you to come,' said Nat firmly, seeing that Prue was looking harried. 'There's plenty of room for you all at Mack River, and you'll always be welcome.'

By the time they left, Cleo and Marisa had planned an entire trip based around the wedding they imagined would be taking place at Mack River, although their knowledge of Australian geography was hazy to say the least. If Prue hadn't been so preoccupied, she would have been amused at the very idea of the two of them in the outback. She couldn't see them tripping around Mathison somehow.

But then, they wouldn't have to. There would be no wedding, and no trip.

As it was, Prue let them plan an itinerary which involved driving from Sydney to Mathison with an overnight stop in Alice Springs and a possible detour to Perth, their increasingly far-fetched ideas flowing over her head. She felt as if she were crouched in a dark place, hugging her new knowledge of how much she loved Nat to herself and terrified in case he got so much as a glimpse of it.

Dreading being alone with him, Prue was tense and snappy as they drove back to the flat. She didn't know how to behave with him any more. She lingered as long as she could in the bathroom, scrubbing her face fiercely as if she could rub away her feelings and go back to the way she had been before, when she had innocently imagined that what she had felt for Ross had been love.

It hadn't been, of course. Prue could see that now. She had loved the *idea* of Ross more than the reality, idealising the fact that he was so good-looking and such fun, and she could live the life she had always dreamt of in a place she loved. She hadn't really known Ross, though.

She hadn't needed him or hungered for him in the way she suddenly, so desperately, did for Nat.

Perhaps it was just a passing phase, Prue tried to comfort herself. She was just obsessing about Nat because they were together, and her feelings wouldn't last any longer than her supposed love for Ross had lasted a few days' separation.

All she had to do was stay calm and not make a complete fool of herself by giving Nat so much as a *hint* that she saw him as anything more than a means to save face with her family, or by doing anything really stupid like throwing herself into Nat's arms and begging him not to let her go. That would only embarrass both of them and make the next few weeks with the twins an agony.

All she had to do, in fact, was to get a grip and wait for this new love to pass.

'What's wrong?' Nat asked when she went back into the bedroom. He was sitting on the edge of the bed, taking off his boots and watching her with a frown in his eyes. She had only spoken in monosyllables since they'd left her parents, and he could feel the tension in her twanging around the room.

'Nothing,' snapped Prue, stalking round to the other side of the bed so there was no temptation to fall weeping into his arms. 'I'm just tired.'

'You've been like this all evening. Didn't you enjoy yourself?'

'Of course I didn't! How do you expect me to enjoy myself when we're stuck in this stupid pretence?'

All of a sudden the fight went out of her, and she slumped down on the bed and put her head in her hands. 'I wish we'd never started this,' she muttered, close to tears. 'It's all so *complicated.* Now we've got my entire family wanting to meet the twins and booking flights out to Australia. Next thing we know, they'll be landing on your doorstop and wondering where I am... Where's it all going to end?' she asked wildly.

'It's going to end when we go back to Australia,' said Nat calmly. He got up and came round the bed to sit next to her. 'There'll be no problem. You can just write to your family later and say that we've decided not to get married after all.'

The longing to lean against him was so great that Prue had to dig her nails into her palms. 'They'll all be so disappointed. You've seen what they're like!'

Nat debated whether he could put his arm round her or not, but decided against it. He didn't trust himself, and anyway she was so tense he felt she might recoil in horror.

'They just want you to be happy,' he said, 'and you will be when you're with Ross again.'

Ross? How could she be happy with Ross when she needed *him*? Prue turned her face away. 'I suppose so,' she muttered.

'I thought you must have been thinking about him this evening.'

'Yes, I was,' she said dully after a moment. She might as well let Nat think that she was still hung up on Ross. Anything other than let him see that all she wanted was to unbutton his shirt and touch her lips to his chest.

Her senses snarled at his closeness. His thigh brushed hers, his arm, and she felt sick and giddy with desire.

'You mustn't let the teasing get you down,' said Nat carefully. 'They don't know how you feel about Ross.'

Prue latched onto the excuse. 'I know,' she said with difficulty. 'I just didn't realise love would be like this.' She swallowed, determined to convince him that she was in no danger of forgetting Kathryn. 'You know what it's like.'

Nat's eyes rested on her averted face. He could see the sweep of her lashes, the tantalising warmth of her skin, the hair curling under her ear. 'Yes,' he said bleakly as he got to his feet. 'I know what it's like.'

CHAPTER EIGHT

PRUE was dreaming a wonderful dream. She was lying on her side and Nat was kissing his way along her shoulder, slow, tantalising kisses to draw her deliciously out of sleep. His hand was at her knee, slipping beneath the cotton nightdress, warm, insistent, irresistible against her thigh.

And, because it was just a dream, Prue could turn with a murmur of pleasure. She could lift her arm to encircle his neck and pull his mouth down to meet hers, and oh! it was so good to be able to kiss him the way she had wanted to kiss him all evening, long, lingering, luxurious kisses that felt absolutely natural and absolutely right.

In a dream, there was no need to pretend. There was no need to think at all. There was just the taste of his lips and the enticing exploration of his tongue and the searing touch of his hands and the feel of his taut, unyielding body pressing hard on hers.

Abandoning herself to a gathering storm of sensation, Prue let her hands roam hungrily over Nat's back. His skin was sleek and supple over solid muscle, and she kissed his shoulder as his lips left hers and travelled possessively down her throat to her breast. She was unravelling, dissolving, feverish in the face of the impatient pulse inside her that clamoured to meet the growing urgency of his hands.

'Please...' she gasped, arching herself towards his touch, incoherent with desire. '*Please...*'

Her pleading filtered through the roar of sensation in

131

Nat's head as if from a great distance. It sounded as if she was begging him to stop and, abruptly wide awake, he stilled in the horrified realisation of what he was doing.

For one endless moment he couldn't move. He lay frozen on top of Prue, his mouth at her breast, his hand on the smooth curve of her hip, until slowly, very slowly, he lifted his head and made himself look down into her face. In the dawn light she looked bewildered, her eyes huge and dark and dazed, and her mouth was trembling uncontrollably.

With a muffled curse, Nat levered himself away from her. He swung his legs over the side of the bed and dropped his head into his hands, swearing under his breath as he fought to bring his body under control.

'What…? What…?' Prue's heart was jerking with shock as she found herself wrenched so cruelly from the dream that had not been a dream at all. She was having trouble forming the words in her mouth while her body was pumping and her mind still spinning. 'What… happened?' she managed to stutter at last.

'I'm sorry, I…' Nat trailed off. How could he explain how he had drifted awake to find his arms around her? Her body had been so warm and inviting. He had breathed in the scent of her skin, of her hair and, half asleep as he had been, it had seemed perfectly natural to kiss the shoulder so temptingly close to his mouth.

And then she had turned, sleepily smiling, and she had kissed him back, and there had been no chance of thinking after that. No chance of realising that she had been too drenched in sleep to recognise that he wasn't Ross after all, until she had begged him to stop—and by then it had been too late.

'I'm sorry,' was all he could say heavily again. He

forced himself to his feet, aware only of the need to re-move himself as far away from her as possible until he could get himself under control.

At the door, he glanced back. Prue was curled up as if from a blow, the duvet clutched defensively around her, and she looked so shocked and vulnerable that Nat flinched with shame. 'I'm sorry,' he said, because there was nothing else to say, and he went out, closing the door very quietly behind him.

Prue was too devastated to move. She couldn't accept how suddenly the glorious dream had turned to cold, hard reality. One moment she had been drowning in enchant-ment, the next Nat had pulled away from her in disgust.

He must have realised too late that she wasn't Kathryn. The only possible explanation broke bitterly through the churning fog of 'whys' and 'if onlys' in Prue's brain.

She could see only too easily how it must have hap-pened. Nat had been in love with Kathryn a long time. He must be used to waking and finding her in his arms, to kissing her awake and making love in the early-morning light. What a shock for him to find this morning that he wasn't at home, and that the woman responding so eagerly and so passionately wasn't Kathryn at all. No wonder he had leapt away from her!

Prue's whole body burned and pulsed with humiliation and unsatisfied desire, and she covered her face with her hands to keep back scalding tears. She couldn't cry. If she cried Nat would know how desperately she had wanted him, and Prue couldn't bear to see the embar-rassment and distaste in his eyes.

Moving stiffly, like an old lady, she got up and with shaking hands pulled on the satin robe Cleo had left hanging behind the door. They couldn't pretend it hadn't happened. She had to go and find Nat right now and

convince him somehow that when she had begged and
pleaded with him to make love to her she hadn't known
what she was doing, or the next three weeks would be
unbearable.

Nat was in the kitchen. Unaware of her at first, he sat
at the table, his head tilted back to stare at the ceiling as
he concentrated on breathing deeply and slowly. Prue
could see the tendons in his throat, the clenched muscles
in his jaw, the faint sheen of sweat on his skin. He hadn't
waited to find a T-shirt, and was still wearing only his
shorts. Prue's eyes rested longingly on his bare chest,
where only minutes ago her hands had drifted so deliciously. She had gloried in the texture of his skin, the
power of his shoulders, the responsive shift of his muscles, and she had pressed her lips to his warm flesh, tast-
ing him, loving him.

And now? Now he was a stranger, out of reach. Don't
look, don't touch. Prue swallowed and clutched the satin
robe together at her throat.

The movement caught Nat's eye, and he lowered his
head slowly until they were looking at each other across
the kitchen.

'I don't know what to say,' he admitted at last.

'You don't need to say anything,' said Prue quickly.
Unsure whether her still trembling legs would support her
much longer, she walked over to the table and sat next
to him.

Her feet were bare and her hair tumbled wildly around
her face. She had no idea how alluring she looked,
thought Nat, close to despair. The dressing gown she was
wearing covered her completely. She was holding it
firmly together at her throat, and all he could see were
her hands and toes, and although that should have made
it easier for him, somehow it didn't.

There was something suggestive about its soft swish as she moved towards him, something tantalising about the way it looked as if it might slide from her shoulders if she let go. The fabric was rich and red, with a slippery sheen. Nat only had to look at it to know how it would slither over her skin if he reached out and touched her.

Which he wasn't going to do, of course. His throat felt like cardboard, and he wrenched his eyes away.

'I don't know what happened,' he said. 'I was asleep one minute and the next....'

The memory of what had happened next flared between them so vividly that they both flinched. 'It caught me unawares,' Nat ploughed on past the constriction in his throat. 'I just...wasn't thinking.'

'I know.' Prue swallowed. 'I thought I was dreaming,' she said, desperate to find some way of explaining why she had responded with such abandon. 'I didn't realise that you...that you weren't...' She stumbled to a halt and looked helplessly at him.

'That I wasn't Ross?' Nat was surprised at how even his voice sounded.

He had offered her the perfect excuse, Prue realised. She longed to be able to tell him that she had been dreaming of him, but how could she do that when she had seen how he had reacted at finding her in his arms?

She nodded dully. It was easier all round if he believed that she had been thinking of Ross. 'I'm sorry,' she said in a low voice, not looking at him.

Her head was bent, and Nat could see the soft nape of her neck where he had kissed her earlier. He wished she had sat on the other side of the table instead of choosing the chair beside him. She looked so miserable that it would be very easy to put a comforting arm around her and feel the shiny robe slip and shift against her skin beneath his hand.

Too easy. Too dangerous.

He clenched his fists instead. 'It wasn't your fault,' he said harshly.

'It wasn't yours either.' Prue coloured painfully. 'We were both half asleep. It was just one of those things.'

The intoxicating sweetness of her kiss. The silken warmth of her body. The excitement blazing between them. *Just one of those things?*

Nat's mouth twisted. 'Just one of those things,' he agreed, and his voice was as dry as dust.

There was an awkward pause.

'I don't want it to change things,' said Prue hesitantly at last.

She twisted the false engagement ring round her finger. 'I know I was in a state last night, but it's been going well, hasn't it? My family are all convinced that we're engaged and the Ashcrofts seem happy.'

Her blush deepened. 'I'd understand if you wanted to tell everyone the truth,' she hurried on, 'but it's only today and tomorrow to get through. Once Cleo and Alex have gone on honeymoon we'll have the flat to ourselves and we can concentrate on the twins. We won't have to…do what we've been doing,' she added lamely.

Nat was just watching her, saying nothing. Unnerved by his silence, and terrified that he was trying to think of a way to tell her that he would rather not have anything else to do with her, Prue rushed on.

'Just now…that didn't *mean* anything. I haven't for-gotten about Kathryn,' she said awkwardly. 'I know noth-ing's going to change the way you feel. But it won't be much longer and we'll be on our way back to Australia with William and Daisy. Once we're there, we can stop pretending and forget all of this. That's what we both want.'

She might want to forget it, thought Nat bleakly. Personally, he didn't think that it would be as easy as that.

'So you want to carry on as we are?' he said.

'Only if you don't mind.' She couldn't tell him that she only wanted to be near him as long as she could. 'I really want to go back to Australia,' she said instead.

Back to Ross.

If he had any sense, thought Nat, he would call a stop to this whole thing now. Somewhere along the line, without quite knowing how or when it had happened, he had fallen in love with Prue and, no matter how hopeless he knew it was, he couldn't find a way to fall out again.

The future stretched drearily ahead of Nat. He didn't know what would be worse, not seeing her at all, or bumping into her occasionally in Mathison with Ross, perhaps married to him, having his children. Wouldn't it be easier to make the break and start getting used to life without her now?

The longer he spent with Prue here in London the harder it was going to be to let her go in the end, Nat knew, but he couldn't bring himself to say goodbye. Not yet. He had promised her a ticket back to Australia, he reasoned. The flight was booked, and he still needed help with William and Daisy. And the next three weeks would be all the time with her he had.

'*Do* you mind?' asked Prue uncertainly as the silence lengthened, and when Nat looked into her grey eyes, he knew that he had no choice anyway.

'No,' he said slowly. 'I don't mind.'

Prue was very glad that there was so much to do that day. Caught up in a whirl of pre-wedding activity, she had her hands full calming Cleo and her mother's last-minute nerves, and she hardly saw Nat, who went off to see William and Daisy again on his own.

In a fit of tradition Cleo had decided to spend the night before the wedding at her parents' house, and Prue as chief bridesmaid was to be there as well. As Alex was to have dinner with his own family, Nat would be left on his own.

'Come home with us,' Cleo urged when Alex pointed this out to her. 'It'll be a bit cramped, but you wouldn't mind sleeping on the sofa for a night, would you?'

Nat smiled and shook his head. 'It's only for an evening,' he said, 'and I'm used to being alone.'

It was true. When Ed and Laura had moved, he had had the homestead to himself and it had never bothered him. If anyone had asked, Nat would have said that he was a solitary man, comfortable with silence and his own company, but that evening in London was one of the longest he had ever spent. He missed Prue with a physical ache. Better get used to it, mate, Nat told himself bleakly.

The sun came out for Cleo's wedding, and it was a perfect day. Prue had often thought the word 'radiant' overused in connection with brides, but it was the only way to describe how her sister looked—as she told her when she kissed her in the church porch before they set off up the aisle.

Cleo hugged her back. 'Your turn next,' she promised.

Except it wouldn't be. Prue forced a smile. 'I hope so,' she said.

She hardly recognised Nat when she saw him standing next to Marisa at the end of the pew. He was wearing a grey suit and tie and an unapproachable expression, and he looked so smart that he might have been a stranger. But then he turned to watch her pacing slowly up the aisle behind her father and Cleo and, catching her eye, he smiled slightly.

His smile was so reassuringly familiar, so *Nat*, that Prue couldn't help smiling back, and as their gazes held the church around them receded and there were just the two of them, just the smile in Nat's eyes and the warm strumming deep inside her.

Mechanically, she kept on walking, and moments later he was cut off from her view, but his smile lingered and she was so absorbed that she nearly bumped into Cleo as she came to a halt beside Alex. Jolted back to attention, Prue stepped forward hastily to take the bouquet.

She watched her sister take her vows, but she was agonisingly aware of Nat at the other end of the pew. If she leant forward slightly she could see his hands, holding the order of service, the same hands that had explored her body so enticingly, and the memory of their sureness and their strength shuddered down Prue's spine and knotted her entrails.

Straightening abruptly, she fixed her gaze on Cleo and Alex once more. What would it be like to be standing where Cleo was standing, radiating happiness, knowing that the man beside her loved her and needed her and wanted to spend the rest of his life with her? Prue let herself imagine Nat turning to smile at her the way Alex had smiled at Cleo. She imagined putting her hand in his and feeling his fingers close around hers. She imagined walking back out into the sunshine with him, going back to Mack River, staying for ever—

A sharp elbow dug into her ribs and she turned to see her mother frowning at her, while the rest of the congregation looked on in some amusement as she was left standing alone with a dreamy smile on her face.

Flustered, Prue sat down abruptly. She had to pull herself together! She had told Nat that she didn't want things to change, but it wasn't true. She wanted them to change completely. He would be horrified if he knew that being a nanny wasn't enough for her any more, that nothing less than marriage and for ever would do.

It wasn't hopeless, Prue encouraged herself. Nat wasn't actually engaged to Kathryn any more, was he? If she could just stay cool and not embarrass him, he might ask her to stay on at Mack River to help look after William and Daisy. Surely if she was there every day he would come to need her? She would make herself indispensable, Prue vowed. She would create a home for the children and cook for him and clean for him and maybe— *maybe*—Kathryn would decide to stay in Perth. And Nat might turn to *her* then. He might come to realise that he needed her, and she would be there for him.

But first they had the next three weeks to get through, and she mustn't spoil things by letting him guess how she felt. For now he just wanted her as a nanny, and a nanny was what she would be. That meant being cool, calm and capable, and *not* the kind of person who was so wrapped up in her daydreams that she had no idea of what was going on around her.

After the service there were hugs and kisses and photographs outside the church. Cleo insisted on including Nat in the family groups, and inevitably he was placed next to Prue.

'Can you get a bit closer together?' shouted the photographer. 'Prue and…Nat, is it?…squeeze up!'

He gestured with his hands to narrow the gap, and they had little choice but to shuffle together. Nat stood slightly behind Prue, so she didn't actually have to look at him, but she could feel how close he was, and the temptation to lean back against him was unbearable. She wanted to take off his tie and his stiff suit, to unbutton his shirt and press her lips to his skin…faint with desire, Prue had to close her eyes.

'OK, smile everyone!' The photographer paused. 'Prue, are you awake? You can't go to sleep yet!'

Snapping her eyes open, Prue fixed a bright smile to her face and clutched her flowers with a kind of desperation. Cool, calm, capable—wasn't that what she had decided? She was going to have to do better than this!

It was easier at the reception. Cleo had decided on a finger buffet rather than a sit-down meal, which meant Prue could avoid Nat as much as possible. If she could just stay away from him, she decided, it would be all right. So she circulated around the room, smiling and nodding and agreeing that yes, it *would* be her turn next, and if sometimes she found herself gravitating too close to Nat, she would turn sharply on her heel, make an excuse and head off in the other direction.

Not that Nat seemed to care—or even notice—*where* she was. Whenever Prue allowed herself to look at him he appeared to be absorbed in conversation, and jealousy would clutch at her heart as she caught a glimpse of his smile. He talked to old aunts and eccentric cousins and friends of the family, all of whom came up to Prue afterwards and told her how much they liked him.

'It's *such* a pity you won't be getting married here,' they sighed wistfully. 'Australia is so far away!'

'I know,' said Prue, and was seized by a longing to be there, in the stillness and the silence of Mack River, a world away from this hotel ballroom with its ornate

mouldings and its swagged curtains and its glittering
chandeliers.

Suddenly claustrophobic, she murmured an excuse and
slipped through the French windows that opened out onto
a long terrace. Leaning on the balustrade, she had taken
several deep breaths before she realised that there was a
knot of children in the garden below. They were clustered
around Nat, who seemed to be showing them a trick of
some kind, for they were all wide-eyed, their gazes riveted to his hands.

Prue leant further over to see what he was doing, and
at the same time Nat became aware of her presence. He
glanced up and their eyes locked.

'Have you escaped?' he asked, and she nodded.

'I needed some air.'

'Come down and join us.'

'Auntie Prue!' Ben came running to meet her at the
steps. 'Nat can do magic with his hands!'

Prue knew that only too well. She smiled down at Ben.
'Can he?'

'Nat, show Auntie Prue what you can do!'

Obligingly, Nat repeated the trick. It was very simple,
but the children were thrilled with it and clamoured for
more, and when he had exhausted his repertoire they
made him tell them about boxing kangaroos and dancing
brolgas, about the flocks of brightly coloured parrots that
wheeled in the sky, about spiders and snakes and the size
of a crocodile's teeth.

Prue sat on the steps in her bridesmaid's dress and
Katie climbed onto her lap to listen to Nat with her. He
talked to the children as equals, and the sound of his
slow, quiet voice was infinitely reassuring. She could feel
the tension ebbing away from her. She hadn't realised
what an effort it had been to avoid him earlier, and now

it was bliss to give in and just be with him for a while. She didn't care that he wasn't talking to her or looking at her or even thinking about her. It was enough to be near him.

Content to sit there quietly, Prue didn't even tense when the children dispersed at last and Nat came to sit beside her on the steps.

'You're their hero now,' she said with a smile. 'Did a crocodile really take a bite out of your boat?'

Nat's eyes glimmered with amusement. 'Maybe it wasn't quite as big a bite as I said,' he admitted, 'but the tooth marks are still there! I'll show you when we get home.'

He stopped, hearing too late his unthinking assumption that Prue would be going back to Mack River with him, but she didn't seem to notice how he had given himself away.

'I can't wait to go back,' she sighed.

She rested her arms on her knees, and watched a plane on its long descent to Heathrow. 'Listening to you just now made me homesick,' she told him. 'I know I was only at Cowen Creek a few months, but it felt like home. I miss the stillness. Everything's so frantic here,' she went on. 'You rush from one thing to the next, and everyone always seems to be in a hurry and you end up so wound up you can't relax at all. I never felt like that at Cowen Creek. It's so quiet there,' Prue remembered wistfully, listening to the babble of voices in the ballroom. 'You can walk along the creek there and there's no one but you and the birds...'

And Ross, Nat reminded himself, seeing how the grey eyes were shining, how her lips curved at the memory of her happiness with him.

Did Ross have any idea of how lucky he was? Nat

wondered with an edge of bitterness. All he had to do was lift a finger and Prue would marry him. He would have a warm, vital, loving wife, a wife to smile and welcome him home at the end of the day, a wife who loved the land as much as he did.

Kathryn had never found the bush romantic. She had a low boredom threshold and, in spite of growing up in the outback, she was much more at home in the city. Kathryn liked people, action, the promise of excitement. Nat couldn't remember her ever wanting to sit and enjoy the stillness and the silence the way Prue would.

Prue would love Mack River. She had seen so little of it on the one day she had been there. Nat wanted to show her the gorge and the waterhole where he and Ed had swum when they were boys. He could ride with her through the canyons and out on the saltpans. They could take swags and camp out in the top end, and he could watch her face at sunset.

Prue had been watching him more closely than he knew. 'Are you thinking of home?'

'Yes,' said Nat. 'Yes, I was.'

Prue could only imagine how pokey and confined London must seem to someone like him. 'Don't you hate being here?'

'No, I don't hate it.' It was true that he felt alien in the city, where he seemed to be moving in slow motion compared to everyone else, and he would be lost if he had to live there, but that didn't mean that he hated it. How could he hate London, when Prue was there?

'You must miss Mack River, though,' she said, unconvinced.

Nat looked into the grey eyes that were silvery in the sunshine. 'Not all the time,' he said. 'Not right now.'

His words hung in the air between them. Prue looked

away and then back, and this time she couldn't tear her gaze away. The air leaked out of her lungs as the silence stretched dangerously, but her body wouldn't obey her increasingly frantic instructions to move, breathe, do *anything*.

'Prue?' said Nat suddenly, as if her name had been forced out of him.

'Yes?'

'I—' He put a hand out, but before he could say any more, her mother's voice was calling down from the terrace.

'*There* you are! I've been looking all over for you two! Do come in. We can't start the speeches without you.'

Perhaps it was just as well, thought Nat as he stood up. He had been about to ruin everything and tell Prue how he felt about her but, judging by the way she had deliberately ignored the hand he had held out to help her to her feet, a declaration of love from him was the last thing she would have wanted to hear.

Prue breathed carefully as she made her way to the front of the crowd gathered around the cake, where her father was waiting with Alex and Cleo, and the best man was nervously going over his notes for his speech.

It had taken every effort of self-will not to take Nat's hand, but she hadn't trusted herself to let it go again. When she looked into his brown eyes like that it was so easy to forget Kathryn and let herself succumb to every instinct in her body that told her she could lean towards him and put her hand to his cheek and kiss him.

But Prue's brain knew better than her body. It remembered how Nat had talked about Kathryn, the things he had said. How much he loved her. It reminded her how appalled he had been that morning when they had so nearly made love. It warned her not to drive him away by betraying how much she needed him.

It wasn't so good at ignoring him as he stood beside her, though.

Her father gave a short, moving speech, and then it was Alex's turn. Most of it flowed over Prue's head. She was watching Cleo, and her throat tightened at the expression on her sister's face as she gazed at her new husband. Cleo looked so happy that Prue felt ashamed, remembering how she had grumbled about coming back from Australia for the wedding. This was Cleo's special day, and she was very glad that she hadn't missed it.

'And finally,' Alex was drawing to a close, 'Cleo and I want to say a special thank you to Prue, who has come a very long way to be here today. We know you had to cut your time in Australia short, Prue,' he went on, smiling at her, 'and we both appreciate it. It wouldn't have been the same for Cleo if you hadn't been here.'

Seeing that Prue's eyes were shimmering with tears, Alex tactfully looked round at the rest of the guests. 'For those of you who don't already know, Prue is going back to Australia to get married, and Cleo and I would like to take this opportunity to congratulate her and Nat and to hope that they will be as happy together as we are.'

'And, just to be sure that you're next,' Cleo chimed in, lifting her bouquet, 'this is for you, Prue. Catch!'

She threw the flowers straight at Prue, who caught them without thinking, to a general cheer.

'To Prue!' they cried, raising their glasses.

Nat was right beside her, and the two of them were the focus of all eyes. They were both very conscious that the natural thing to do would be to kiss. It was a wedding, they were supposed to be in love, everyone was drinking to their future happiness. How could they *not* kiss?

Prue's eyes lifted to Nat in mute appeal. Resigned to his fate, he smiled slightly to show that he understood, put an arm around her, and dropped a brief kiss on her lips, his mouth barely grazing hers before he drew back.

There, that wasn't so hard after all, was it? Nat congratulated himself.

Prue didn't know whether to be relieved or disappointed that the kiss was over almost before it had begun.

Relieved, she decided firmly after a moment. It had been fine. She hadn't fallen apart and she hadn't made a fool of herself, and she could even smile her thanks to Cleo and wave the bouquet as if she had nothing more on her mind than picking a suitable date for her wedding.

'Thank goodness that's over!' said Prue, collapsing onto the sofa when she and Nat finally made it back to the flat that evening. She kicked off her shoes with a groan and lay back.

'I was beginning to wonder if Cleo and Alex were ever going to go,' said Nat, following her into the sitting room.

For some reason, things were easier between them. It was as if getting through that very public kiss had been a watershed. It had been so brief, so impersonal, that there had been no danger of either of them losing control.

Of course, it was a bit late *now*, Prue couldn't help thinking with an inward sigh. The celebrations were over, and they wouldn't be put in that kind of situation again. There would be no need for Nat to kiss her when they were just here with William and Daisy, but it was reassuring to know that if they *did* have to she could trust herself not to go to pieces the way she had done before.

Nat, too, was conscious of an easing of tension, but he

was still careful to choose a chair where there would be no danger of touching Prue accidentally.

Loosening his tie with a grimace, he unfastened his constricting collar. 'It beats me how people can wear suits every day,' he said. 'I'm not going to need it again, am I?'

'No, you've done your bit.' Prue massaged her toes and watched him as he leant back and ran his hands through his hair in a gesture of weariness. 'Thank you,' she said impulsively.

Nat lifted his head slightly and cocked an eye at her. 'What for?'

'For everything you've done this week,' she said. 'For saving my face and being nice to my family and wearing a suit and...' For not making it obvious that you wished it had been Kathryn that you were kissing. 'For everything, really.'

Nat's brown eyes were unreadable. 'It was a pleasure,' he said.

'Yes, well...' Prue cleared her throat. 'I just wanted to say how much I appreciated everything you've done. You've kept your side of our bargain, and now I'm going to keep mine. From now on, I'm just here to look after William and Daisy.'

CHAPTER NINE

'THAT'S the lot.' Nat dumped the last of the carrier bags on the table. He couldn't get used to toiling up a flight of stairs to get to the kitchen.

'You survived, then?' Prue looked up smiling from the floor, where she was kneeling with Daisy and letting her help put the potatoes away in the bottom of the vegetable rack.

It had been Nat's first solo drive through London traffic to the vast supermarket by the Thames and he had claimed to be setting off with some trepidation, although Prue knew that he would manage it in the same competent way he managed everything else. It would take more than London to intimidate Nat.

'Just,' he said, scooping up William, who had been holding up his arms and babbling for attention. 'There was a point somewhere near the cheese section when I wondered if I would ever see daylight again, but I used my tracking skills to find the checkout, and after that all I had to do was find the car again.

'Do you have any idea how many cars there are parked in that place, William?' he asked, holding him at arm's length and looking him in the eye.

William looked back, wreathed in smiles. He loved being part of a conversation. 'A—*bah*!'

'That's right…thousands. I reckon you could put the whole of Mathison in that car park six times over. The general store will never be the same again!'

Prue laughed as she got to her feet. 'I'd rather shop

there any day,' she said, brushing down her knees. 'No, darling!' She rescued the tomatoes as Daisy made a lunge for something new and more exciting. 'You stick with the potatoes and carrots. You're doing such a good job.'

Successfully diverting Daisy by shaking a few more root vegetables out of a bag, she put the tomatoes safely out of reach and began unpacking the other bags that Nat had placed on the table.

'Do you remember driving me to the store that day?' she said to Nat, who had shifted William onto one arm and was setting the bulk packs of disposable nappies to one side.

Nat remembered all right. He remembered the tears on her lashes, how desperate she had been to win Ross's approval. *I'm in love with him*, she had said. *He's the only man I'll ever want.*

'I remember,' he said, although there were times when he looked at Prue—holding out her arms to the babies, catching them to her, blizzarding kisses over their faces until they squealed with delight—and it was all too easy to forget.

'It seems ages ago, doesn't it?'

Prue found it hard to believe that it was barely six weeks since she had buried her head in her arms and wept because of Ross. She had been so sure that she loved him but now when she tried to conjure up his image, all she got was an impression of merry blue eyes and virile energy.

Whereas Nat… She could draw every line of his face with her eyes closed. She knew exactly how his hair grew at his temple, the precise point at which the crease in his cheek deepened when he smiled, and if anyone had asked her to identify just where the pulse-beat was in his throat, she could have pointed to it with unerring accuracy.

'A lot's happened in the last few weeks,' Nat agreed, rather muffled through William's hand, which was patting his mouth. 'We've come a long way since then.'

She might have moved geographically, thought Prue ruefully, but emotionally she was back where she had started, hopelessly in love with a man who was probably never going to be interested in her.

'I guess when you flagged me down on the Cowen Creek track you didn't think that six weeks later you would be knee-deep in babies,' Nat went on.

'No,' Prue admitted. She had been unable to think about anything except Ross then. It was like remembering a different person, another life altogether.

Nat hesitated. He set William down next to Daisy, who wasn't sure if she wanted her brother interfering with her game. She shouted a protest, but William ignored her. He placidly picked up a carrot and stuck it in his mouth and after a final suspicious glare, she returned to the enthralling business of putting potatoes into the rack and then taking them out again.

Having waited to make sure that William was balanced and not at risk of a shove from his sister, Nat turned back to Prue.

'I have to say that I'm very glad you forgot to check the fuel before you left Cowen Creek that day,' he said slowly.

He had spent the last few days on a very steep learning curve, and was adapting pretty quickly considering that he hadn't known one end of a baby from another before he left Mack River. Now he could change a nappy in his sleep, although he was still ham-fisted compared to Prue. She made everything look easy, even at meal times—deeply messy affairs—when she would pop a spoonful of food into the baby's mouth and wipe off the drips while the spoon Nat offered was as often as not knocked imperiously aside.

'I wouldn't have been able to manage without you,' he told her honestly.

The least sign of approval, and Prue was reduced to blushing like an idiot! 'I'm glad I forgot too,' she admitted. 'I love being with William and Daisy.'

And with you, she added mentally.

She looked down at the pair of them, each absorbed in their own play and unaware that there was anything more fascinating than the taste and texture of the humble vegetable.

'They're gorgeous babies,' she said wistfully, wondering if there would ever be a time when she would have babies of her own, babies like Daisy and William with fat, dimpled wrists and Nat's brown eyes.

'They seem to love you, too,' said Nat, thinking of how quickly the twins had accepted Prue.

She was very loving with them, cuddling them in her arms and laughing as they threw themselves against her and gave her wet sloppy kisses with their open mouths. She let them suck her nose and stroke her hair and pat her mouth until she caught their little hands and kissed their palms. Nat would find himself watching her sometimes, and was uncomfortably aware that he was jealous of his own niece and nephew.

'You're a natural mother,' he said, and Prue's eyes met his with an almost startled look.

'I'd like to be,' she said quietly, hoping that he hadn't been reading her mind.

There was a pause.

Nat cleared his throat and his mind of a picture of Prue with a tiny baby in her arms. *His* baby, not Ross's. 'I hope this girl from the agency is as good as you,' he said, and Prue froze in the middle of stacking butter in the fridge.

'What girl?'

'Didn't I tell you? I rang the agency in Darwin yesterday to see if they'd found anyone to come to Mack River as nanny and housekeeper when we get back.'

A cold hand closed over Prue's heart. 'No, you didn't tell me,' she said expressionlessly.

'It was when you were out buying those books.'

Nat had made himself ring. However much she loved the babies Prue wouldn't want to stay with them for ever, he had reminded himself, and sooner or later he was going to have to face the fact. She had made it very clear that she was hoping to be able to go back to Cowen Creek and, if that was what she wanted Nat couldn't stand in her way, however much *he* loved *her*. She deserved the chance to be happy with Ross.

By making other arrangements for someone to help him with William and Daisy he had hoped to show Prue that he wasn't expecting any more of her than what she had agreed, which was to accompany him and the babies back to Mack River. She hadn't said that she would stay, and he couldn't ask her to unless she was sure there was no chance of returning to Cowen Creek.

'I see.'

Prue had had a wonderful time in the bookshop. Nat had given her *carte blanche* to buy a whole stock of books and toys to send out to Mack River for William and Daisy as they grew up. She had imagined reading the stories to them, watching their little faces as they puzzled over their first words, and she had let herself get so carried away that she had forgotten that chances were she wouldn't be there to read anything.

Nat hadn't forgotten.

She turned back to the fridge. 'What did the agency say?'

'They've got a girl who sounds nice, but she can't start until after Christmas, so I've asked them to keep looking.'

Prue's fingers tightened around a block of cheese at the idea of a *nice* girl effectively moving in with Nat. She would try and accept it if Kathryn came back to make him happy, but she didn't see why she should let some unknown girl, however nice, make herself indispensable to him. That was *her* plan.

And it sounded as if she only had until Christmas to put it into action.

'I could stay until then if you wanted,' she said as casually as she could.

It was Nat's turn to still. 'I thought you wanted to go back to Cowen Creek?'

'I haven't heard anything from the Grangers. Their new cook must be settled in by now, and she'll probably be there until the end of the season.'

Prue risked a glance at Nat. 'You *did* say I could stay at Mack River until I found another job,' she reminded him, hoping that she didn't sound too desperate, 'and I just thought that since Daisy and William already know me, it might work out for both of us if I stayed on as their nanny for a while.'

'Are you sure?' Nat could hardly believe his luck.

'I'm sure,' said Prue. She concentrated on slotting the milk into the fridge door. 'I was dreading saying goodbye to William and Daisy,' she said to explain her willingness to throw Cowen Creek to the winds and base herself at Mack River instead.

'That would be…' Fantastic. Wonderful. Glorious. Superb. 'That would be good,' said Nat. 'I'd pay you, of course,' he added hastily. 'Whatever you wanted. And if you do get a chance to go back to Cowen Creek, Prue, then you just have to tell me. I'd let you go whenever you want.'

It wasn't quite what Prue wanted to hear, but she was elated at the thought that she would have at least another three months with him. A lot had happened in six weeks, as Nat had pointed out. How much more could happen in three months? Three months was plenty of time for Nat to forget about Kathryn and nice girls who wanted to be nannies.

And in the meantime she could relax and enjoy this strange time out of time. They had nothing to do but look after the twins, and the long, hot summer days were passing lazily. Prue would have been frantic if she had had to cope on her own, but somehow it was easy when Nat was there. He was never impatient and he never flapped or looked harassed.

It hadn't taken them long to fall into a routine. Prue had been afraid that it might be difficult being alone together in the flat after Cleo and Alex had gone, but in the event they had both been too tired to feel self-conscious at all.

They'd set up the cots in Cleo's room, where Prue now slept in solitary splendour in the wide bed. The obvious thing would have been to put them in the spare room, and give the twins a bedroom of their own, but that would have involved continuing to share a bed, and in view of what had happened the last time they slept together neither of them had wanted to suggest it.

William and Daisy had been unsettled by the change for the first few nights, and one or the other of them had woken up several times a night, generally waking the other in the process. Prue and Nat had both been up with them at all hours.

There was an intimacy about being awake together in the still of the night. London was enduring a heat wave, and Prue was too hot and too tired to bother with a robe. It was bad enough wearing a nightdress, and she envied Nat, who wore shorts to preserve the decencies but could hold a baby to his bare chest as he walked up and down. Prue was sure that William and Daisy picked up on his slow heartbeat and were soothed by it.

Cradling the other baby, she would sometimes watch enviously and wish that she could relax against him and be held that securely, but generally Prue had felt that she was coping pretty well with being alone with him in the dark with hardly any clothes on. It should have been an awkward situation, but there was no time to think about awkwardness when you had two screaming babies on your hands and when desire came a long way down the priority list after the longing for a few hours of uninterrupted sleep.

By the time the twins had settled down into sleeping through the night, Prue had convinced herself that things would be fine. And they *were* fine, most of the time. As long as she didn't brush against Nat by accident, or make the mistake of looking into his eyes when they laughed, or notice how strong and gentle his hands were when he held the babies.

If she avoided all of these things, getting through the day was no problem at all. Daisy and William woke her with their singing in the morning, and she lifted them out of their cots to play in the bed with her. Nat would bring her a cup of tea, which she never got a chance to drink, as the twins lurched precariously between them, demanding to be kissed and cuddled and bounced on their knees.

It was impossible to be constrained when they wanted to play peek-a-boo behind their hands or to have their tummies tickled until they chuckled with glee.

After their morning nap, Prue and Nat would take them out. Sometimes they went back to see their grandparents and to play in the garden there, and a couple of times they visited Prue's parents.

The days Prue liked best, though, were the ones when the four of them were alone and they caught a red bus into the great parks at the centre of the city. 'You might as well see London while you're here,' she'd said to Nat, although sometimes when they sat with the twins gurgling on their laps and drove past the famous landmarks it felt as if she was the one seeing London properly for the first time.

The parks were littered with people stretched out and enjoying the sunshine, but Nat had a much warier attitude to the sun and insisted that William and Daisy wore floppy hats and sat in the shade. Propped up against them, the babies were fascinated by everything going on around them. There were so many people for them to look at and so much going on that they were never bored.

Prue lay in Green Park one day and looked around her. It was another beautiful day, with just a few cirrus clouds adrift in the sky, and a soft breeze carrying the smell of cut grass and sunshine lifted her hair. Daisy nestled against her, happy to rest for a moment, and William was sitting between Nat's knees, absorbed in stroking the grass. Prue couldn't remember ever feeling as relaxed in the city before.

'London doesn't seem so bad on a day like today,' she said, closing her eyes with a contented sigh.

Absently steadying William, who was wobbling as he reached for a leaf, Nat watched the way the dappled light from the broad leaves above fell across her face. Daisy lay on her stomach, her head on Prue's breast and Prue's hand on her padded bottom, holding her securely. The two of them looked utterly relaxed. The corners of Prue's mouth were curved upwards and the long dark lashes swept her cheek, hiding the beautiful grey eyes.

Nat made himself look away. 'I hadn't realised there were places this green in the middle of London,' he said. Picking a blade of grass, he chewed it thoughtfully. 'We could do with grass like this at home.'

'They were muttering about drought on the news last night,' said Prue without opening her eyes.

'Drought?' Nat looked incredulously around him at the sweeping, freshly cut grass and the lush green trees, and he remembered the bitter times at home when the rains failed and the dust blew over the empty paddocks. 'They don't know what drought means!'

He was silent for a while, thinking about Mack River and imagining what was happening on the station. 'They should be mustering this week,' he said, half to himself.

Prue opened her eyes to look up at him. He was holding William between his hands and gazing down to where the traffic roared ceaselessly past Buckingham Palace, but she knew he was seeing something very different: a place where there were casuarinas and gums and boab trees instead of sycamores and chestnuts, and where there was no traffic and no tourists and no men in suits striding briskly past, barking orders into their mobile phones.

'It's not a good time for you to be away, is it?' she said.

Nat shrugged slightly. 'It can't be helped. The ringers know what they're doing, and Bill Granger promised he'd keep an eye on things while I'm away. Right now, William and Daisy are more important.'

'It won't be for much longer anyway,' said Prue. 'Cleo and Alex will be back from their honeymoon soon, and we can go home.'

She had spoken without thinking but now her words with their implied intimacy seemed to echo around them. *We can go home.*

But Mack River wasn't her home, Prue reminded herself sadly. Biting her lips, she glanced at Nat to see if he had noticed her casual assumption that she would belong at Mack River with him and found herself looking right into his deep, brown eyes.

He had noticed all right, she thought with a tiny jump of her heart. He was watching her with a strange expression and as he opened his mouth, Prue was suddenly convinced that he was about to point out that she was going to Mack River as a nanny and nothing else.

'Back to Australia, I mean,' she said quickly, before he could speak.

What else? Nat turned away dully, shaken by how close he had come to revealing exactly how he felt.

We can go home. It had sounded so right when Prue said it, as if the two of them were meant to be together. As if she belonged with him at Mack River, as if there was no question that she would go back with him and stay for ever.

'We'd better tidy the flat before Cleo and Alex get back,' was all he said.

Prue heard the constraint in his voice without understanding what had caused it. 'We'll need to have packed by then anyway,' she said, sounding as awkward as he did now. 'We fly out the evening after they come back.'

Now was not the time to remind him that they would have to share a bed again for the night they overlapped with Cleo and Alex, but the prospect clanged in Prue's brain.

An uncomfortable silence fell. Nat gazed unseeingly at a girl who was managing to roller-blade and talk on the phone at the same time, and tried to forget the image of Prue at home at Mack River.

He wished he couldn't picture her there quite so clearly. He could visualise exactly how she would look sweeping the verandah, stopping to smile a welcome as he came up the steps, waking in his bed. If only she hadn't looked so right amongst his furniture.

'Ga!' William's shout made Nat start. He had forgotten his nephew was there for a moment.

The baby was waving his arms excitedly, and when Nat looked around he saw instantly what had attracted his attention. A police horse was making its way slowly along the path and, glad of the diversion, Nat hoisted William up and carried him over so that he could see better.

Easing the sleeping Daisy gently onto the grass, Prue sat up and watched them. She couldn't hear what Nat was saying to the policeman but she saw him run a hand down the horse's nose and whisper to it. The horse stood still, its ears flickering as if it were listening. It was a huge animal, but William was quite unafraid. He reached out a chubby hand and stroked its coarse mane, and then Nat let him feel the horse's velvety lips and warm breath.

When the policeman moved on with a smile, William let out a wail of disappointment. 'Don't worry, Will,' said Nat as he carried him back to join Prue and Daisy on the grass. 'There are plenty of horses at Mack River. You'll be riding your own one day soon.'

Together they watched the horse moving sedately away, its tail twitching. 'You and Daisy will each have a pony of your own,' Nat promised William. 'Would you like that?'

'Baba!' William's shout sounded so much like enthusiastic agreement that Prue couldn't help smiling.

'You would?' Nat turned his nephew round and held him between his strong hands so that they faced each other. 'Then when you're big enough, you can help muster the top end,' he said, talking to him as seriously as if William could understand every word. 'It's rough country up there, and nothing beats a man on a horse when it comes to tracking down those scrubber bulls.'

'Gah, gah, ma?' said William, so thrilled at participating in a real conversation that his intonation rose just as if he had asked a real question.

'Too right,' said Nat. 'Daisy'll come too. We'll take our swags and sleep on the ground, and we'll build a fire and make damper and drink billy tea, just like your dad and I did when we were kids.'

Prue's heart twisted. She could imagine them so clearly, the man on his horse with the two children riding beside him, their faces bright and alert. She could see the firelight on their faces and the glimmering stars above them, but she couldn't see herself.

She wouldn't be there.

Beside her, Daisy stirred and knuckled her eyes. Prue picked her up and cuddled her on her lap until she woke properly and then let her have a drink, kissing the top of her head while she guzzled thirstily.

Daisy's wispy hair was clean and soft, and Prue breathed in her baby smell. Daisy wouldn't be riding for a while yet. For now, she still needed Prue.

Glancing up, she caught the eye of two middle-aged women who were passing and they smiled at her. 'What lovely babies,' one said, looking from the unusually an-

gelic Daisy to William, who was clambering happily over
Nat. We must look like a perfect family, thought Prue
wistfully.

'You are lucky,' the other woman said, and all she
could do was smile weakly back at them as they walked
on.

Lucky? Perhaps she was at that, Prue decided. The
future might be unclear, but this time next week she
would be at Mack River with Nat. When William and
Daisy were in bed, and the men had eaten and gone back
to their quarters, she and Nat would be alone in the dark
outback night.

Things could be worse, Prue reminded herself, and felt
much better. Things could be a lot worse.

The phone rang when they were giving Daisy and
William their lunch the next day.

Expecting her mother or Marisa, Prue tilted back in
her chair and groped for the cordless phone which she
had left on the worktop behind her with one hand, while
with her other she deftly slipped another spoonful into an
unsuspecting William.

Nat shook his head in admiration. He was engaged in
a battle of wills with Daisy, who was being particularly
naughty, and the resulting mess was smeared and splat-
tered over both of them, not to mention the floor around
her highchair.

'Behave yourself, Daisy,' scolded Prue as she pressed
the 'receive' button on the phone, but she was smiling
as she lifted it to her ear. 'Hello?'

'Prue? Is that you? It's Ross.'

Prue nearly dropped the phone. Abandoning William's
lunch, she had to put both hands up to hold the receiver.
'Ross?' she croaked, and Nat looked up sharply.

'Yeah, it's me! I called your parents and they gave me this number.' Ross's vigorous voice came surging down the line, so clear that he might have been in the next room. 'How are you doing?'

'Fine,' stammered Prue, who was totally unprepared for this. 'Fine,' she said weakly again.

'I bet those babies are a handful! Nat's not working you too hard, is he?'

'No…no, everything's…fine.'

It wasn't very original but it was the best she could do under the circumstances. She glanced at Nat, but he was carefully scraping around the edge of Daisy's bowl and apparently not paying any attention to her conversation.

'That's great,' Ross was saying. 'Listen, Prue, I rang to ask when you'll get back to Mathison.'

'Next Thursday, I think.'

William was mindlessly shoving an empty spoon in his mouth. Prue leant forward and automatically filled it for him. Pleased, he took it and proceeded to wave it around energetically. Most of the food fell onto his bib but the spoon made it to his mouth eventually, so he seemed to be getting the idea.

'Why, there's not a problem, is there?' she asked, trying to keep her mind on the conversation.

'We've got a bit of a crisis in the kitchen,' Ross confided. 'You know that girl who was so keen to come and work in the outback when you left? She lasted a couple of weeks and then got fed up and went off to Cairns. We're all hoping that you'll come back, Prue. You're the best cook we've ever had.'

'I don't know, Ross…'

Prue was finding it difficult to concentrate, what with William's erratic spoon and Daisy, who was banging her hands in her dish and vociferously protesting at Nat's attempts to get some food down her.

And Nat, with that wooden expression, pretending he couldn't hear what Prue was saying.

'Don't say no!' Ross was at his most charming. 'We all want you back.' He lowered his voice. 'Especially me.'

'I…it's a bit difficult.'

Leaving William to it, Prue pushed back her chair and got up so that she could turn her back on all the distractions. 'I did say I'd stay on to look after William and Daisy, and I don't want to leave Nat in the lurch.' She tried to explain to Ross without letting him or Nat know how desperate she was to go to Mack River. 'He can't manage two babies on his own.'

'Oh, he won't be on his own,' said Ross cheerfully. 'That was another reason I rang—to drop a word in Nat's ear that a certain someone close to his heart is very keen to get back together with him again!'

Unaware of Prue's heart splintering at the other end of the line, he chatted on confidentially. 'Kathryn's been asking when Nat's coming home, and I think she wants to meet him at Mathison. She made me promise to ring her with the flight details as soon as I had them. Between you and me, I reckon she's come to her senses at last and realised that she won't find anyone like Nat down in the city.'

Every word was like a knife turning inside her. Prue felt sick. Why, why, *why* had she let herself carry on dreaming about Nat when she had known about him and Kathryn? Why had she let herself believe that Kathryn would stay conveniently in Perth? Of *course* she would want Nat back in the end.

'I see,' she managed past the constriction in her throat.

'So, what do you say, Prue?' said Ross eagerly. 'Nat won't need you if he's got Kathryn to give him a hand, will he?'

'No,' said Prue in a voice dull with pain. 'No, he won't.'

'But *we* need you at Cowen Creek. I tell you, meals haven't been the same since you left! You did say you wanted to come back if you could,' he reminded her when she didn't jump at the offer.

Prue couldn't deny it. There had been a time, a lifetime ago, when it was all that she had wanted. She wouldn't be here now if she hadn't dreamt and hoped and prayed that Ross would ring her up and say just what he was saying.

'Yes, I did,' she agreed.

It seemed that she had little choice. As Ross had pointed out with such unintentional cruelty, Nat wouldn't need her any more. Even if he asked her to stay on for a while to ease William and Daisy into their new life at Mack River, Prue didn't think she could bear to see him happy with Kathryn. At least Ross was offering her a chance to keep her pride intact. It wasn't much of a comfort, but it was all that she had.

With an immense effort, Prue forced a smile. 'When you put it like that, how can I refuse?' she said. 'I'd love to come back.'

'Great! I'm looking forward to seeing you again. I missed you, you know.'

'I've missed you, too.' What else could she say?

She heard Ross give a muffled exclamation. 'Before I forget, can you give Nat a message from Dad when you see him?'

'You can tell him yourself. He's right here.'

Pinning a bright, brittle smile to her face, Prue turned and offered Nat the phone. 'I'll finish feeding them if you want to take it in the other room,' she said. 'Ross wants to talk to you. He's got some good news for you.'

CHAPTER TEN

'THAT was good news, wasn't it?' Prue flashed Nat a brilliant smile as he came back into the room and put the phone very carefully back onto its cradle on the wall.

'Yes, very.'

Once Nat had got rid of the phone, he didn't know what to do with his empty hands. He stood by the wall, looking down at them and trying to remember exactly what Ross had said. There had been something about Kathryn, but all he had taken in was that Prue wasn't coming back to Mack River with him after all. She was going to Cowen Creek, and to Ross.

So, yes, it was good news for her.

Nat knew that he should make the effort to sound pleased for her, even if his own future did yawn bleak and empty. 'Ross sounds very keen to get you back,' he managed.

'Yes.' Prue wished that she could sound more enthusiastic.

She finished wiping up the mess around Daisy's chair and straightened. She didn't want to look at him and see the happiness in his face at the thought of seeing Kathryn again, so she went over to the sink instead and rinsed out the cloth with unnecessary vigour.

Nat saw the unconscious slump of her shoulders and sudden hope flickered. She didn't seem *that* happy. Maybe she wasn't as desperate to go back to Ross as he had thought. 'Are you OK?' he asked.

Prue's betraying back snapped back to attention, and

by the time she turned she had her smile in place once more.

'Of course,' she said brightly. 'Ross has missed me and they want me back at Cowen Creek. It's just what I wanted to happen when we left.'

It wasn't what she wanted now, though, but she couldn't tell Nat that. It wouldn't be fair on him to complicate matters when he was about to sort things out with Kathryn.

Nat's brief hope died, and he was left with a dull, empty feeling inside. 'I'm glad it's worked out for you.'

'I'll miss William and Daisy, though,' said Prue, in case he had seen past her smile to the desperation in her eyes. He obviously expected her to be over the moon, and the babies provided a good enough excuse for not doing handsprings around the kitchen.

It was true, anyway. Picking up William, she hugged him against her shoulder and kissed the side of his head. The thought of saying goodbye to him and his naughty sister made her heart crack.

'You're going straight back to Cowen Creek from Mathison, then?' asked Nat after a moment.

'I might as well.' Prue put William on the floor and turned to lift Daisy, who was leaning out of her high chair and protesting loudly at being left behind. 'After all, you won't need me if Kathryn's there to give you a hand.'

How could he tell her that he would always need her? It would only make her feel guilty about leaving him with the twins, and that wouldn't be fair. She had done what she promised to do, and now she deserved the chance to be happy with Ross.

'No, we'll be fine,' said Nat a little too heartily, and was unable to resist adding, 'The kids will miss you.'

But not as much as he would.

'They'll soon get used to me not being there,' said Prue. She swallowed. 'I'm sure they'll love Kathryn.'

Kathryn... Nat remembered the cryptic message Ross had passed on. Ross seemed to believe that Kathryn was ready to throw up her life in Perth and come back to live with him at Mack River, but to Nat, who knew Kathryn better than anyone, it sounded highly unlikely.

He couldn't even imagine Kathryn at Mack River now, and he certainly couldn't see her giving up her career to wipe dirty faces or change nappies or clear up after Daisy had finished eating. She would play with the babies, and no doubt charm them the way she charmed everyone else, but Nat was pretty sure that she would lose interest the moment they became less than adorable.

Still, Ross had said that she was determined to meet him at the airport, and he might find that he was glad of her help. However fastidious she might be, Kathryn was a friend, and she wouldn't let him down if he needed another pair of hands. She would make it easier to say goodbye to Prue, too. He could pretend to be glad for her if he had Kathryn as an excuse for not throwing his pride to the winds and begging her to stay with him.

Prue was never sure how she got through those last few days in London. She kept a fixed smile on her face, but inside she felt as if she were shrinking away from her bones as misery churned in her stomach and clawed at her heart.

There were endless goodbyes to get through, too. Her father hugged her and told her that Nat was a fine man, her mother sent her off with much grandmotherly advice about dealing with the twins, and Marisa made her promise to let them know the wedding date as soon as possible so they could book their flights to Australia.

It was even harder leaving the Ashcrofts for the last time. Ruth clung to her when it came time to say good-bye.

'I can't tell you what a difference it makes to know you'll always be there for Laura's children,' she said tearfully. 'Harry and I know we're doing the right thing letting Daisy and William go back to Australia with you and Nat. You'll be a good mother to them. We can trust you and Nat to love them and look after them for us.'

Harry Ashcroft hugged her tightly as well. 'If Laura could see you, she would approve,' he said gruffly. 'She would have liked you very much.'

Prue swallowed the hard lump in her throat. 'I'm glad,' she said.

'You'll come back and see us some time with William and Daisy, won't you?'

There was the tiniest of pauses and then Nat spoke. 'Of course we will,' he said.

Prue wiped her eyes as they drove away, the twins babbling cheerfully in the back, oblivious to all the emotion. 'I hope we did the right thing,' she sighed. 'Ruth and Harry are going to be devastated when they found out that we lied to them. When will you tell them the truth?'

'What truth?'

'That we're not really in love.'

'Oh, that truth,' said Nat. His voice was remote, the way it had been ever since Ross had rung. 'I'll leave it a few months and then write to them. I'll just say things didn't work out. If the twins are safe and happy I don't think they'll mind too much.'

Cleo, brimming with happiness and brown and glowing from her honeymoon, took them to the airport.

'I wish you could stay longer,' she said. 'I've hardly had a chance to talk to you since we got back.'

Knowing how quickly her sister would sniff out anything wrong, Prue had deliberately avoided spending any
time alone with her. 'I'm sorry, Cleo,' she said as she
hugged her goodbye. 'We have to go back.'

'I know.' Cleo held her tightly. 'Thank you for coming, Prue. I used to think that you were making a terrible
mistake going to live in the outback and taking on two
small babies, but I was wrong. You and Nat are absolutely right for each other.'

At last it was over. They handed over their passports
to be checked, passed through security control and there
was no more need to pretend.

They barely spoke on the long flight to Singapore, and
what conversation they had was limited to the twins. The
airline provided sky cots for the babies, and they slept
most of the way, which left Prue nothing to do but be
achingly aware of Nat, silent and withdrawn beside her.
For someone returning to his first and only love he was
very subdued, Prue thought, but then he had always been
a private man. Perhaps he had always worn that unapproachable expression, and it was only now that she was
sensitive enough to notice?

Prue remembered the last time they had boarded a
plane together, how hopeful she had been, how thrilled
at the prospect of returning to Ross. Didn't they say that
you shouldn't wish too hard for what you wanted in case
you got it?

She sighed and turned to face the window. Outside
there was only darkness and the monotonous drone of the
engines. Maybe she could recapture that longing, she told
herself.

Maybe she would take one look into Ross's blue eyes
and fall in love with him all over again. He was much
more suitable than Nat, anyway. He was her own age, he

was handsome, he was fun. She got on well with his parents and loved his property. What more could she want?

Maybe in a few days' time she would marvel that she could ever have thought that Nat was the one she loved.

Maybe.

As the jumbo began its slow descent to Singapore, Prue looked down at the ring on her finger and remembered how little it had meant when Nat had bought it for her during the last stopover. It had taken her ages to get used to seeing it on her hand, but now it seemed to belong there.

Not any more. Taking a deep breath, she tugged the ring off her finger and held it out to Nat. 'You'd better have this back,' she said. 'I don't need to wear it any more.'

'You might as well keep it,' said Nat after a single, curt glance.

'Oh, but I couldn't—'

'What use is it to me?' he interrupted harshly. 'I'm not planning on any more pretend engagements. It's just a cheap ring,' he dismissed it. 'Keep it as a souvenir.'

Prue's fingers closed around the ring so tightly that the stones dug into her flesh. 'Thanks,' she said bitterly.

Nat clearly had no wish for a souvenir of the time they had spent together, but then, why would he? He had Kathryn to go home to, and she probably already had a beautiful engagement ring. Kathryn wouldn't be interested in the cheap little diamond that had been good enough for *her*. Prue wished that she had the pride to throw the ring away, but she knew that she would keep it. Soon it would be all of Nat's that she had left.

It was an interminable journey, but part of Prue didn't want it to end. When it ended she would have to face the hardest goodbye of all, and every hour that passed was an hour less she had to spend with Nat. Secretly, she hoped for a delay somewhere along the line, but they made all their connections easily. The Darwin flight left bang on time, and by the time they had shuffled through immigration at the other end the local plane which would take them on to Mathison was already waiting on the tarmac.

Both William and Daisy were fed up with travelling by then, and unimpressed by the smaller, noisier plane that linked a number of small outback towns. They grizzled and wriggled and cried at the pressure on their ears as the plane landed.

Mathison was the third stop. As they took off for the last time, Prue held a struggling Daisy in her lap. Only half an hour left. Her heart was drumming and there was a cruel band of steel tightening around her throat and making it hard for her to breathe.

Twenty five minutes…twenty… The seconds ticked inexorably away, and all too soon the plane began its descent over the familiar scrub. Prue could see Mathison below her, a cluster of buildings squeezed together by the vast, empty red country around it. There was the hotel, there was the store where Nat had driven her that day they had met, and now there was the airport….

The plane was sinking fast. Seconds later, it had bumped down onto the Tarmac and was speeding along the runway, its engines screaming, while Daisy provided the counterpoint.

Trying in vain to shush her, Prue looked out of the window. She could see the tiny terminal building and the cluster of people waving behind the rail. Ross would be there, and Kathryn.

This was it then. It was over.

Numbly, she carried Daisy, still yelling, down the steps. The heat hit her like a blow. Mingling with the aircraft fumes, it wavered over the Tarmac and refracted the light so that the terminal and the waiting people seemed to hover above the shimmering ground.

Nat had William in one arm, and their cabin baggage in the other. Without speaking, they walked across the Tarmac towards the barrier.

A beautiful girl with long legs and a mane of auburn hair was smiling and waving. Prue knew without being told that it was Kathryn. She made everyone else look faded and dowdy, and her smile was dazzling. Bitterly, Prue remembered how she had dreamt of making herself indispensable to Nat, of being there when he turned to her, of replacing Kathryn in his heart. How presumptuous she had been to imagine that he could forget someone like Kathryn!

Kathryn's face was alight, and she pushed her way towards him as he came through the barrier, calling his name. Prue had to watch as, not thinking how William might feel at a strange woman throwing herself at him, Kathryn flung her arms round Nat's neck and kissed him.

'Oh, Nat, I couldn't wait see you again!' she cried.

William's little face puckered and he burst into tears. Disentangling himself from Kathryn with a muttered apology, Nat put down the bag and joggled the baby against his shoulder. His heart sank as he saw Kathryn's slightly hurt expression, but he couldn't deal with her and a crying baby. Instinctively, Nat looked around for Prue.

He was just in time to see Ross put an arm round her and hug her to his side. 'Welcome back,' he was saying, smiling down at her with his dancing blue eyes.

Wiser than Kathryn, Ross made sure that he didn't

crowd Daisy, but he tickled her on the tummy with a grin. 'G'day, there!'

Daisy was so surprised that she stopped crying abruptly and stared at him, and, under Nat's jaundiced gaze, she dissolved into smiles. She was obviously no more immune to Ross's charm than any other female, Nat thought, watching sourly as his niece flirted her lashes and chuckled as he tickled her again.

Seeing that William had redoubled his cries, Prue handed Daisy to Ross. 'Would you mind holding her a minute, Ross? I think Nat needs a hand.'

'Hi!' Kathryn turned her warm smile on Prue as she went over. 'You must be Prue!' She winked. 'Ross has been telling me *all* about you!'

Prue managed a brief smile before turning to Nat, who was still trying to quieten William's wails. 'Why don't I take him?' she said, holding out her hands. 'That'll give you two a chance to say hello properly.'

Without waiting to see Nat take Kathryn in his arms, Prue carried William into the shade and found a quiet corner to sit down with him and cuddle him reassuringly until he calmed down. He had subsided into hiccupping little sobs when Kathryn came to join her on the seats. She had apparently inherited a smiling Daisy from Ross, and sat jiggling the baby on her knee.

'Ross has gone with Nat to sort out the luggage,' Kathryn told Prue with another friendly smile. 'Nat was muttering something about putting special seats in the car, so I guess they might be a little while. He said I'd frightened William too,' she said contritely, and chucked his chin. 'Sorry, William!'

From the safety of Prue's arms, William was prepared to concede a smile.

'It's just a bit confusing for them,' Prue apologised.

'I know, it was thoughtless of me. Nat's always told me I don't stop and think,' said Kathryn cheerfully. 'I was just pleased to see him again. I've got so much to tell him! I must say,' she added, cocking a curious eyebrow at Prue, 'he does seem a bit uptight. I've never seen him so grumpy before. Has he been like that the whole time?'

'It's been a long flight,' said Prue stiffly.

She wished Kathryn wouldn't be so nice. She wanted to hate her, not to find her warm and open and confiding. Kathryn was chatting about Ross now, asking how long she had known him and saying how much she would be envied by the other girls in the district.

'He certainly sounds very keen!' she said with a wink. 'When we were waiting for your plane to arrive he didn't stop talking about you and what a wonderful cook you are, and you know what they say about the best way to a man's heart...!'

It had obviously never crossed Kathryn's mind that she might have any reason to be jealous, or that there could be anything between her and Nat, Prue thought sadly. And there wasn't anything. They had made a deal, and they had both kept their side of the bargain, and now it was over.

Nat and Ross reappeared at last. Ross was grinning, but Nat had a set expression that only hardened when his eyes fell on Prue. 'Sorry about the wait, but we're ready now,' he said almost brusquely. 'Only one more leg, kids, and then we're home.'

He stood in front of Prue and looked down at her. 'I think it would be better if you and Ross went first. I'll take William.'

Nodding dumbly, Prue got to her feet. She held William tightly against her for a moment, kissing his chubby hand. She wanted to say goodbye but she couldn't speak, so she just gave him to Nat and bent to kiss Daisy on her wispy curls, wishing that there was some way of telling them how much she was going to miss them.

Now all she had to do was say goodbye to Nat. Straightening, Prue drew a ragged breath and made herself look at him. 'Will you let me know how they're getting on?' she asked unsteadily.

'Of course.'

She managed a wavering smile. 'I'll say goodbye, then.'

'Goodbye, Prue.' On an impulse Nat bent and kissed her cheek, a warm, fleeting kiss that seared her to the soul. 'Thanks,' he said. 'Thanks for everything.'

Somehow, Prue made herself turn and walk away beside Ross, but she had only taken three steps when Daisy and William, belatedly realising what was happening, set up a wail. It took everything Prue had not to turn back to them, and she had to cover her ears with her hands, unable to stop the tears spilling down her cheeks.

'They'll be fine once you've gone,' said Ross hearteningly. 'Out of sight, out of mind.'

Out of sight, out of mind. Prue only wished that it were true. The Grangers had welcomed her back with flattering warmth and put down her subdued spirits to jet lag. They were so kind that Prue felt guilty that she couldn't be happier to be back. She threw herself into the cooking to try and keep the pain at bay but, far from fading out of her mind, the longer she was away from Nat and the twins, the more she ached to see them again.

She tried everything to forget Nat. She told herself that it had been the equivalent of a holiday romance, that it hadn't been real, that she had only fancied herself in love because they had been thrown into such an intimate situation. She reminded herself that he was happy and didn't need her. She did her best to fall back in love with Ross.

None of it worked. Ross, intrigued at first by her preoccupation, soon lost interest once it was obvious that the days of her uncritical adoration were over. When she had an hour off, Prue would walk down by the creek where she had used to go and dream about Ross. Now she dreamt about a very different man, a quiet man with slow hands and a slow smile.

She yearned to see him again. Several times she picked up the phone to ring Mack River just so that she could hear his voice, but each time she put down the receiver before she had finished dialling. She could have asked how Daisy and William were, but he had promised to let her know, and if he hadn't contacted her it must be because he had better things to do. When was it going to get any easier? Prue wondered in despair. She couldn't spend the rest of her life with this raw ache inside her. Sometimes it felt as if someone was pulling her entrails out of her, loop after loop.

It was nearly two long, bleak weeks before she had any news from Mack River. Prue was drearily setting out the lunch and wondering how much longer she could stand it when Joyce Granger came back from Mathison, big with news.

'I met Bev Martelli in the store,' she said, unpacking the groceries Prue had asked her to get while she was in town.

'Who's she?' asked Prue without much interest.

'I thought you'd know her,' said Joyce, surprised. 'Her husband is the married man at Mack River.'

Prue's head came up abruptly. 'Oh?' she said, dry-mouthed.

'She reckons Nat Masterman is having a bad time with those babies.' Joyce shook her head. 'He can't get a nanny to stay. The first one left after three days, and the next only managed a week, so now he's trying to cope on his own until he can find someone else. Bev does what she can, but she's got three kids of her own and all the cooking to do.'

'But…what about Kathryn?' asked Prue, clutching the knives and forks to her chest. 'I thought she would be there.'

'Well, so did we. We were all sure that the engagement was on again, but I don't think it can be. Bev said she went back to Perth as soon as the first nanny turned up.'

Prue could only stare at Joyce, unable to take in what she was saying. Kathryn had *gone*? Why? What had happened?

'Of course, I got on the radio to Nat straight away,' Joyce was saying. 'I said why didn't I send you over to help him out, since it sounded like he needed you more than we did, but Nat wouldn't hear of it. He said he could manage.'

'Manage?' said Prue in slowly gathering wrath as Joyce's words sank in. 'How can he possibly manage the two of them on his own and run a cattle station?'

'You know what men are like. They won't accept they need help.'

Prue slammed the cutlery down on the table. 'He should be thinking about William and Daisy, not his own stupid pride!' she said furiously.

Two weeks she had endured the agony of not seeing him, and all the time she could have been at Mack River! All Nat had to do was ask, but no! He had let her break her heart with wanting him and rung up his stupid agency instead!

Prue was so angry she didn't know what to do with herself. All those tears, all that pain he could have spared her if he had simply picked up the phone and asked for her help! She didn't know whether it was Nat's lack of consideration for the twins' comfort that enraged her or his refusal to turn to her when all she had wanted was a chance to love him but, whichever it was, it had jolted her out of her misery.

'I must say, it's not like Nat,' Joyce commented mildly. 'He's usually so level-headed.'

'He's just being stubborn and stupid and pig-headed!' snapped Prue, invigorated by the rage scalding through her. She untied her apron and threw it over a chair. 'Mrs Granger, can you manage without me for a few days? I'm going to ask Ross to fly me over to Mack River right now!'

'Does Nat know you're coming to stay?' Ross grinned as she threw a small bag into the back of the plane and climbed into the seat beside him. The propeller of the small Cessna was already whirring.

'No,' said Prue, tight-lipped, 'but I'm staying whether he likes it or not!'

No one knew that she was coming, so there was no one to meet her at the airstrip but it wasn't far to the homestead. Clutching her bag in one hand, still buoyed up by anger, Prue marched along the track.

She could hear the bawling before she got halfway across the yard. Stalking up the verandah steps, she slammed through the screen door, dumped her bag and headed straight down the corridor to the source of the noise.

William and Daisy's combined lung power drowned
out the sound of her footsteps and Nat was unaware of
her presence as Prue paused in the open doorway. She
derived some satisfaction from seeing that the calm, con-
trolled Nat was looking distinctly harassed at last.

He was struggling to change William's nappy and casting increasingly desperate glances over his shoulder to
the cot where Daisy had whipped herself into a pitch of
screaming frustration.

'Hold on, Daisy,' he pleaded. 'I'm just coming.'

Daisy's face was bright red and screwed up with misery, her eyes piggy with tears. She looked, thought Prue,
exactly the way *she* had been feeling for the last two
weeks.

And that was Nat's fault, too.

Exasperated, Prue went over to the cot and picked up
the screaming baby. 'Shh, shh, sweetheart,' she whispered.

Nat, fumbling with the nappy and still deafened by
William's bawling, had yet to notice her, but he regis-
tered the diminution in the volume as Daisy responded
to the familiar feel of Prue's arms and burrowed into her,
the screams subsiding to mere heart-wrenching sobs.

'Good gi—' Nat stopped as he risked a glance over
his shoulder and saw Prue, cradling Daisy in her arms.

'It's all right now, it's all right,' she was murmuring
soothingly. 'I'm here now.'

'Prue?' he croaked, half afraid that he might have con-
jured her up out of his imagination. '*Prue*…!' She had
to be real. She *had* to be. 'Prue, what are you doing
here?'

'What does it look like I'm doing?' she snapped. 'I've
come to help.'

She seemed angry, thought Nat, still reeling with shock

and consumed by the sheer joy of seeing her again. He couldn't take his eyes off her as she carried Daisy over and laid her on the changing mat next to William's.

'Prue...' He couldn't seem to say anything else. He wanted to pull her to him, to run his hands all over her to convince himself that she was real, to devour her with kisses, but she was deftly stripping Daisy of the dirty nappy and her expression was decidedly stormy.

'How long have things been like this?' she demanded, jerking wipes out of the box.

Nat didn't pretend not to understand her. 'Three days,' he said. This wasn't the way he had imagined seeing Prue again but, as she was being so efficient with Daisy, he might as well finish changing William.

'The last nanny couldn't cope. She said Daisy and William were too much for her, although I was doing as much as I could. I asked her to stay until I could find someone else, but she wouldn't. The agency is supposed to be sending another girl out in a few days. I thought I could manage.'

'Do you call this managing, with both of them screaming their heads off?'

'I'm doing my best,' said Nat, faintly defensive.

'It's not enough!' Prue's hands moved automatically while inside she was shaking with a mixture of fury and emotion at just being near him again. 'Why didn't you ask me to help, Nat? You must have known I would come!'

Jaw set, Nat finally managed to fasten William's nappy. He snapped the Babygro together and lifted his nephew against his shoulder, patting his back until his outraged screams subsided like Daisy's, although he continued to snivel into Nat's neck.

Nat was very tired. He had hardly slept for the last two

weeks. It had been a nightmare trying to deal with the two of them single-handed. He hadn't realised how much he had relied on Prue. William and Daisy were miserable and unsettled without her, and so was he. He had missed her desperately.

'Why didn't I ask you?' he repeated, an undercurrent of anger stealing into his voice. If she only knew how many times he had reached for the phone! 'I didn't call you because I didn't want you to feel that you had to leave Ross as soon as you'd got back. You went on and on about how much you loved him and how all you wanted was to go back to Cowen Creek. I thought the last thing you'd want was to be dragged away to help me.'

'I'd have done *anything* to come!' Prue was so angry at his obtuseness that she was almost shouting. 'I only went with Ross because I thought Kathryn was going to be here. Couldn't you *see*...?'

There was an astounded silence, broken by the last hiccuping sobs of the babies. Appalled at how badly she had given herself away, Prue stared into Nat's shocked brown eyes for a long moment before her fury evaporated without warning and she began to cry.

She put her hands up to cover her face and gave in. 'Oh, Nat, I've missed you so much!' she wept.

Nat's first reaction was helplessness. Now he had three of them in tears, and only two arms. He was looking between them, wondering which of them needed him most, when he belatedly realised just what she had said. She had missed him.

'Prue,' he said in a shaken voice.

'I'm sorry, I'm sorry.' Prue turned hastily away and was trying to change Daisy and wipe her cheeks at the same time, but the tears wouldn't stop. 'I didn't mean to tell you like this, but all I wanted was to come here and be with you, and then Mrs Granger said you didn't want me.' Her voice broke again.

'Not want you?' Nat almost laughed. 'Prue, I've wanted you ever since you kissed me on the verandah here.'

Prue's hands stilled on the nappy and her head turned to him very slowly, as if it had been pulled round on a string. 'You have?' she whispered.

Nat shifted William into one arm, and reached out his free hand to pull her gently towards him. 'Come here,' he said softly, and she leant into him with a sigh of release, circling him with her arms and pressing her face into his throat. 'Shall I tell you how much I want you, Prue?' he said into her hair. 'Shall I tell you how much I've missed you too?'

His arm tightened around her. 'Shall I tell you how much I love you?'

'Yes,' said Prue, lifting her face to his. 'Oh, yes, please!'

Their mouths found each other in a kiss that was honeyed with promise but all too short. It wasn't easy to kiss the way they both wanted when William was smacking Nat's hair crossly and Daisy was objecting equally loudly to the loss of attention.

Reluctantly, Nat let Prue go. 'How do you tell a nine-month-old to shut up?' he asked with a resigned sigh, and she laughed, high on the enchantment that was fizzing and flooding through her.

'You don't,' she told him. 'I'll finish Daisy and then we'll give them a drink. Perhaps that will keep them quiet for a bit.'

They sat on the double seat on the verandah, a baby on each lap. William and Daisy guzzled contentedly and at last a blissful hush descended. Nat put his free arm around Prue. 'Tell me again how much you missed me,' he said with a smile.

Frustratingly one-handed as it was, it was a much better kiss this time, deep, and hungry and intoxicatingly sweet. Breathless at last, Prue kissed her way along Nat's jaw and down his throat before resting her face there and breathing in the scent of his skin.

'I love you,' she said, muffled against him, and Nat slid his fingers under her chin so that he could tilt it and kiss her again.

'I wish I'd known,' he said when he could speak. 'Why didn't you tell me?'

Prue leant her head against his shoulder and thought how right it felt to be there, with his arm around her and the warm, solid weight of a baby in the curve of her body. 'I thought you were in love with Kathryn.'

On Nat's lap, Daisy choked and spluttered and Nat sat her upright, rubbing her back. 'I only let you think that because I thought it would be easier for you,' he said.

'*Easier*?'

'You were so full of Ross,' he explained. 'I thought you might feel awkward if you knew that I was falling hopelessly in love with you, so I pretended I was hoping that Kathryn and I would get together again, but it wasn't true. Kathryn and I have always been good friends but I've never loved her the way I love you, and she knows that.'

'But Ross said—'

'Ross got the wrong end of the stick,' said Nat. 'He was right about Kathryn wanting to see me as soon as I got back, but it was only because she wanted me to be the first one to know she was getting married to a man she met in Perth. We'd been engaged for a while, and she wanted to tell me herself so that I didn't hear about it through the grapevine. It was typical of her to come all the way up here, but she got more than she bargained for—if she wasn't dealing with babies she was listening to me talk about you! I'm not surprised she headed back for Perth as soon as the emergency nanny arrived!'

'We've wasted so much time,' sighed Prue, snuggling happily against him. 'I was so certain you were in love.'

'I was,' said Nat, smoothing her hair behind her ear and kissing it. 'With you.'

They shared another blissful kiss.

'You'd better ring your family tonight and tell them to book their tickets,' he murmured against Prue's lips. 'Say we'll get married as soon as they can get here.'

Prue laughed softly as she kissed him back. 'We don't need to get married straight away,' she pointed out. 'My visa lasts a year and I'm not going anywhere now!'

'I'm not waiting any longer than I have to,' said Nat firmly.

Removing Daisy's bottle from her slack grasp, he propped her against his shoulder and patted her gently to wind her. 'Besides,' he went on, rewarded by a burp, 'do you have any idea how hard it is to get nannies to stay in a place like this? I want to make sure you're on a permanent contract!' His brown eyes were teasing. 'After all, I reckon I'm getting a bargain—a cook, a nanny and a wife all rolled into one. There's no way I'm letting you go now!'

Prue's eyes shone silver with happiness. 'So you'll tell the agency you don't need that nice girl they've booked for you any more?'

'I'll ring them this afternoon,' promised Nat. 'I'll say I've got the only nice girl I need. There's only one cook I'll ever want and only one nanny' He kissed her again. 'And absolutely, definitely, only one wife!'

A year of royalty...

Harlequin Romance®

HIS MAJESTY'S MARRIAGE

Two romantic royal novellas by
award-winning authors:

Lucy Gordon
and
Rebecca Winters

June 2002 (#3703)

He's powerful, privileged and passionate—but the
woman he wants...is the one woman he can't have!

And don't miss:

THE PRINCE'S PROPOSAL
by Sophie Weston
July 2002 (#3709)

She's an ordinary twenty-first-century girl...
forced to be a princess for a year!